The Wedding Season

Reese, Cassie, Gina and Marnie were best friends.
Until *that* night.

They haven't seen each other in years, but
now Reese is getting married and she
wants everyone there.

It will be a reunion to remember—and the wedding
of the year! But what these feisty women haven't
reckoned on are the sizzling, scandalous, and
very surprising consequences…

Don't miss this fabulous quartet from your
favourite Modern Tempted™ authors—
Aimee Carson, Amy Andrews, Heidi Rice
and Kimberly Lang.

The Unexpected Wedding Guest by Aimee Carson
Available July 2013

Girl Least Likely to Marry by Amy Andrews
Available August 2013

Maid of Dishonour by Heidi Rice
Available September 2013

Marnie's Story by Kimberly Lang
Available October 2013

D0785821

Also by Heidi Rice

Too Close for Comfort
One Night, So Pregnant!
The Good, the Bad and the Wild
On the First Night of Christmas…
Cupcakes and Killer Heels
Surf, Sea and a Sexy Stranger
Unfinished Business with the Duke

Heidi Rice was born and bred and still lives in London. She has two boys who love to bicker, a wonderful husband who, luckily for everyone, has loads of patience, and a supportive and ever-growing British/French/Irish/American family. As much as Heidi adores 'the Big Smoke', she also loves America, and every two years or so she and her best friend leave hubby and kids behind and *Thelma and Louise* it across the States for a couple of weeks (although they always leave out the driving off a cliff bit). She's been a film buff since her early teens, and a romance junkie for almost as long. She indulged her first love by being a film reviewer for ten years. Then a few years ago she decided to spice up her life by writing romance. Discovering the fantastic sisterhood of romance writers (both published and unpublished) in Britain and America made it a wild and wonderful journey to her first Mills & Boon® novel.

Heidi loves to hear from readers— you can e-mail her at heidi@heidi-rice.com, or visit her website: www.heidi-rice.com

This and other titles by Heidi Rice are available in eBook format—check out www.millsandboon.co.uk

To my partners in crime—
Aimee Carson, Kimberly Lang and Amy Andrews—
for being such fabulous authors, such an inspiration to
work with and such cool women to boot.
We rock, ladies!

PROLOGUE

Hillbrook College Campus, Upstate New York, ten years ago.

'IT SOUNDS AWESOME, Marnie, but Carter and Missy shouldn't get overwhelmed by all the glamour of their wedding and forget the important part—that they love each other.'

Reese's words of whimsy drifted into Gina Carrington's consciousness—through the cloying perfume of hyacinth blossoms that infused the back porch, and the haze of one too many glasses of vintage champagne—and didn't improve her melancholy mood one iota.

Can we get off this topic now, please?

Her cheeks heated as a heartening flash of temper pierced through the hollow feeling of loss that had dogged her for days. Ever since she'd made the biggest mistake of her life. And in a life filled to bursting with mistakes of one sort or another that was quite an achievement.

'That won't be a problem. They're devoted to each other and they have been for years. When Carter proposed, Missy and I stayed up all night talking about how wonderful it was that we'd be sisters for ever.' Marnie laughed at her own observation, the high musical lilt clearing the fog from Gina's head like a knife slicing through flesh.

Funny to think she'd once enjoyed the sound of Marnie's laugh. Marnie had been so anxious and serious and unassertive when she'd first arrived at Hillbrook. It had taken them all a while to realise her perfect Southern manners had actually been a disguise for extreme terror. Gina had loved hearing that smoky laugh in the months that followed because it had come to symbolise Marnie's emancipation from the people she herself had described as 'the family that feminism forgot'.

But Gina wasn't loving it much now.

'So what's Missy's dress like?' Reese asked, still humouring her.

'Just so perfect,' Marnie purred, her Southern accent thicker than molasses. 'It's ivory silk. She's going to be a traditional bride.' Marnie flashed a smile Gina's way. 'I know not everyone here approves, but I think it's so romantic that her and Carter have decided to stay pure until their wedding night.'

Wasn't it just.

Gina's stomach heaved up towards her breastbone as she plopped her champagne flute on the porch table. 'Is anyone getting another bottle? I'm not sure I can stand to hear any more about love's young dream without alcoholic fortification.'

Cassie jumped up from her seat on the rail. 'It's gotta be my turn,' she said in her broad Aussie accent. 'I'll go.' She sent Gina a bland look that only made Gina feel more miserable.

Cassie knew what had happened a week ago when Marnie's big brother Carter Price had come to visit. And in typical Cassie fashion had been completely pragmatic about it. *'I don't see why you should feel guilty—he's the one that's engaged to be married.'*

But as Cassie headed off to the kitchen, obviously keen to escape from the tension that had been building all night and only Marnie seemed oblivious to, Gina knew Cassie the super nerd felt uncomfortable. And while Cassie would never judge her, Gina knew it took a lot to make Cassie uncomfortcal contact with his fiancée—so desperate to be touched it had almost made Gina cry the way he'd responded with such enthusiasm to a simple kiss and actually thanked her in that slow Southern drawl when she'd pulled down his zipper and placed her palm against the firm, resilient flesh of his erection. She hadn't realised then that he'd been a virgin, but when he'd admitted the truth afterwards, as they'd been lying in the heady rush of afterglow, his voice embarrassed and reticent, it had made her heart squeeze tight in her chest.

To realise that a man so virile, so handsome and so sexually curious had denied himself the most basic of human connections because the woman who was supposed to be his soul mate had demanded it of him... What kind of woman could be that clueless about the man she was marrying? And how cold and judgmental and frigid did you have to be to even want to?

The harsh laugh that came out of her mouth didn't sound like her, but somehow it fitted with who she was now: the Evil Sex Queen sent to split up the happy couple and then slink back into the dark forest of regrets and recriminations.

'Actually your good friend Missy hasn't talked to Carter about the *marital act*, but tell her not to worry.' The two-hundred-dollar champagne soured in her belly. 'As it happens her groom has a natural aptitude for bringing a woman to orgasm. Not only is he hung like a stallion, but he's also exceptionally dexterous, remarkably flexible and really goal-orientated. I should know—I road-tested him myself.'

'*What?*' Marnie's choked sob of distress was accompanied by Reese's spurt of shocked laughter.

'Gina, will you quit teasing her? It's not funny.'

'If that's supposed to be a joke, it's in really poor taste,' Marnie said, sounding like a child having a temper tantrum—naïve and judgmental and impossibly young, the way Gina had never been. 'Missy would be heartbroken if Carter broke his vow,' Marnie finished and Gina could have sworn she heard the rest of the sentence reverberating in her head.

Especially with a tramp like you.

Gina suddenly felt painfully sober, the buzz of alcohol clearing to make her feel reckless and vindictive. Carter had walked away from her determined to throw himself on the mercy of the Virgin Queen—but she wasn't going to keep his secret. Because she wasn't ashamed of what they'd done. She wasn't ashamed of the pleasure they'd shared, and she refused to regret the connection they'd made. It had been real and valid, even if it was only ever meant to be for one night.

'Don't upset yourself, Marnie.' Reese patted Marnie's back, as her mother hen tendencies came charging to the fore. 'It's just Gina's British sense of humour.' Reese sent her a quelling look, that held a trace of censure, but a much bigger trace of confusion. 'Stop being so cynical, Gina, and tell her the truth. I don't know what's gotten into you tonight.'

Gina heard the exasperation in Reese's voice and knew exactly what had gotten into her friend, the Park Avenue Princess, because it was written all over Reese's face, and had been ever since she'd returned from her trip to New York for their final night together. Reese had fallen head over designer heels for that marine she'd met in some diner. She'd seen Reese caressing the dog-tags under her shirt, when she thought no one was looking. And she'd announced earlier in the evening that Mason was 'The One'… As if she were quoting a line from one of those fluffy chick flicks she often forced them to endure on movie nights.

Bitterness and something that felt uncomfortably like envy scoured Gina's throat, making her want to hurt Reese too.

Reese the hopeless romantic, who actually believed in love at first sight. Thank goodness she'd never be daft enough to believe such an idiotic concept. Any more than she'd be dumb enough to fall for Marnie's dictates on the 'proper way to conduct a committed relationship'.

'Actually, Reese, the only thing to have gotten into me is Carter Price's stallion-like—'

'Stop, don't say any more,' Marnie shouted, covering her ears like a child that didn't want to hear the truth. 'It's not true. It can't be.' But Gina could tell the truth had sunk in as tears leaked out of Marnie's eyes. 'You're lying. Carter wouldn't do something like that. He has integrity. And he loves Missy.'

'He may love Missy, but he made love to me.'

'Gina, you didn't,' Reese whispered, hugging Marnie now, her confusion replaced with sadness and concern. 'How could you do something like that? You knew he was engaged.'

Because I talked and he listened. And he talked and I listened. And we touched and kissed and held hands and it meant something. Because he was smart and funny and tender and when he looked at me I felt sexy and special, instead of sexy and shallow.

But she didn't say any of those things, because they weren't really true. It had just been an illusion conjured up by the sultry summer night and the heady pheromones that had intoxicated them both—and it had all disappeared by morning. So she said the thing that had been true all along—before she'd gotten tripped up by feelings that she now knew she should never have trusted.

'I did it because he was hot and he was begging for it. Why do you think?'

Reese swore softly. While Marnie jumped to her feet, her face contorted with anger and disgust. 'But he's engaged to be married. Don't you have any honour at all? How could you be such a…such a tramp?'

Gina forced herself not to flinch. She'd been called a tramp before; in fact, she'd been called a great deal worse than that by her own father. But it was the first time it had been said by someone who meant something to her.

'She's not the tramp,' Cassie announced as they all turned to see her with the newly opened bottle of champagne frothing over her fingers. 'She's not the one who was engaged to be married. He is. Blaming Gina for his infidelity is just another example of the double standard that—'

'You *knew*?' Marnie interrupted Cassie before she could get into full feminist lecture mode.

'Yes. She told me the morning after it happened.'

'Why didn't you tell me?' Marnie cried, the emotional outburst in sharp contrast to Cassie's calm, unblinking stare.

'Why would I tell you? It was between Carter and Gina.'

'Because Carter's my brother and his fiancée is my best friend? Because I'm going to be her maid of honour. Because this is a disaster.' Marnie collapsed back into her seat. 'I can't tell Missy. She'll be devastated. The wedding's in a week's time. And Missy's devoted herself to planning it for over a year.'

'Don't worry, he's not cancelling anything,' Gina supplied. 'He went back to her, didn't he?' She inspected her nails, battling the clutching pain in her chest as she maintained the charade that it didn't matter, that she didn't care. 'I don't know why you're getting so worked up, Marnie. It was nice while it lasted but I didn't want to keep him.'

'I can't believe I respected you. I liked you. I thought you were cool. When all you really are is a lying tramp who has no heart and no scruples.'

'You got it in one, Scarlett.' Gina stood up, taking the opened bottle from Cassie. 'I'm the tart with no heart.' A phrase she'd heard so many times from her father—and had always believed until a week ago, when her heart had put in a surprise appearance.

She inclined her head towards the now dark athletic track,

the buff male bodies they'd had so much fun admiring together over the months now gone for good. 'Looks like the
show's over for tonight, so that's my cue to leave.' She sloshed
a final slug of Reese's priceless champagne into her glass and
toasted them all. 'It's been a ball, but I'm off. I've got an early
start in the morning for the flight back to London.'

'Wait a minute, what about our road trip?' Cassie asked,
her eyes as round with concern as Reese's now. 'We're booking it tomorrow, remember?'

'I'll take a rain check on that.' She nodded towards Marnie, who was staring at her as if she had snakes instead of hair
sprouting out of her head. 'Right at the minute, I'm thinking
I'd rather not spend three weeks in a car with Scarlett staring daggers at me.'

She strode back through the house, Marnie's harsh words
and Reese's concerned buzzing fading as she concentrated
on keeping her back ramrod straight and the self-pitying urge
to cry on lockdown.

Cassie caught up with her on the stairs. 'Gina, I don't get
it. You can still come on the road trip. Marnie will get over it.
What her brother did with you really isn't any of her concern.'

But just as she finished saying it the high, angry shout of
'whore' echoed through the house, making them both stiffen.

Gina pressed her hand to Cassie's cheek. And wondered
how her friend could be so scary smart and yet so clueless
about the most basic of relationship dynamics?

'We'll see. I'll speak to you tomorrow. See how me and
Marnie feel then.'

But she already knew, Marnie wasn't going to forget it.
Gina had made absolutely sure of that. Once again, she'd
burned her bridges. Pushed the people away who mattered
so she wouldn't have to let them mean that much. She already
regretted her outburst. The cruel, outrageous, provocative

things she'd said. But it was too late to take them back now. And it was probably better that way.

She wasn't any good at friendships. And the three of them needed to know that.

Cassie nodded. 'All right. I'm really going to miss you, you know.'

I'll miss you too. And Reese and even Marnie.

But instead of admitting that much, Gina simply nodded and walked away.

She called a cab the next morning before anyone was up. Happy with the deliberately flippant parting note she'd spent several hours before dawn composing.

Sorry for screwing up our last night together so royally, Awesomes. But I think we all knew, me and my insatiable appetite for man candy were bound to mess things up at some point. I hope you can forgive me.
G x

CHAPTER ONE

New York City, August, the present.

> *Something's come up. U & M will have to pick fabulous venue for Cassie's do without me. C u tomorrow at Amber's Bridal. 11a.m. Don't B late. R xxxx*

'REESE MICHAEL, I am going to murder you.' Gina Carrington glared at the text that had popped up on her smartphone.

This was a set-up, pure and simple.

Now her old college roomie was in the throes of second-chance nirvana with her sexy ex- and soon-to-be new-husband Mason, Reese was so full of the joys of spring—and Gina suspected really spectacular sex—that she was starting to make Pollyanna look like a killjoy.

The something that had come up was Reese's cock-eyed optimism, and leaving her and Marnie to have this meeting without her was her unsubtle way of getting them to kiss and make up properly after that fun-filled night a decade ago when they'd hurled words such as 'Tramp' and 'Whore' and 'Virgin' at each other before busting up the Awesome Foursome.

Gina's fingers hovered over the keypad of her phone as she cursed her own stupidity.

She should have seen this coming, as soon as Reese had

suggested that the three of them organise a surprise wedding
party for Cassie and Tuck, the hot jock she was scheduled to
marry at the Manhattan Marriage Bureau on the Friday before Labor Day.

But the truth was, Gina hadn't given it a second thought.
Reese was classy, committed to her friends and a champion
organiser—the original Park Avenue Princess—it had made
total sense that she would come up with an idea like this.

In typical Cassie fashion, their super-geek friend had
agreed to marry Tuck and then left the arrangements up to
him. No fanfare, no fuss, no debauched fun or inappropriate
frolics had been either planned or discussed. So after speaking
to Tuck, Reese had decreed the three of them should handle
that part of the programme without telling Cassie. Because
Cassie would go into a geek-induced coma if they made too
much fuss, they had opted to celebrate in understated style—
inviting the minimalist guest list that would be witnessing
the wedding at City Hall to a great meal at a great restaurant
right after the event.

Hence the decision to meet at this ungodly hour of the
morning in Gina's favourite diner near Grand Central Station
and debate possible venues, before booking one.

But Reese being Reese had seen a way to turn what should
have been a polite and straightforward affair, with her as
the official gooseberry, into a peace-keeping mission of UN
proportions.

Gina and Marnie had remained civil to each other, meeting again for the first time a little over a month ago, during
the fiasco that was Reese's Wedding-That-Wasn't to Dylan
Brookes—the original Mr Too Perfect. That should have
been enough, Gina thought resentfully. They had spoken to
each other, they had even joked with each other in a strained
way. No insults had been hurled, no punches thrown, no eyes
gouged out, which in Gina's mind was a result. But clearly,

that hadn't been good enough for Reese, who was now a fully loved-up member of the sweetness-and-light club. Reese wanted all the dirty laundry properly aired and then washed clean—so the four of them could go back to being the carefree college roomies who'd hit it off instantly at Hillbrook College.

But to Gina's way of thinking, that simply wasn't ever going to happen. You couldn't go back and undo the mistakes you made. You simply had to learn to live with them. And she didn't think that Marnie would ever forgive her. Because she hadn't yet forgiven herself.

Not only that, but kissing and making up with Marnie would involve talking about a man Gina had promised herself she wouldn't even think about again, because she'd thought about him far too often in the intervening years. Namely, Marnie's big brother, Carter Price. The man she'd had one wild night with just weeks before his wedding day. A wild night the consequences of which had not only nearly destroyed her but, from what Reese had told her, had managed to screw up his life rather comprehensively too.

Gina's newly manicured nails tapped out a tattoo on the side of her smartphone as she glanced at the ornate clock on the diner's far wall—and the urge to quickly text Marnie and make her excuses increased. She still had ten minutes to do a runner before Marnie arrived—because for the first time in recordable history she was actually early.

Sighing, she locked her phone and slung it back in her bag. Ten years ago she would have gone with the urge—and run out on Marnie and the unpleasant conversation that loomed large in her foreseeable future. Because when she was nineteen, doing whatever took her fancy and then running away from the fallout had been her speciality. She smoothed damp palms over the vintage dress she'd picked up in a thrift store in Brooklyn a week ago. How inconvenient that she wasn't that reckless, irresponsible tart any more.

'Can I get you something, miss?'

Gina pasted a smile on her face at the helpful enquiry from the college kid who was waiting tables.

'Something hot and strong would be good,' she said, checking him out from force of habit.

His fresh face flushed a dull red. 'Umm... What did you have in mind, miss?'

'Coffee,' she said, taking pity on him as the flush went from pink to vermillion. 'And this morning I'm going to need it neat.

He nodded. 'Coming right up.'

She watched him stroll off and smiled.

While she might not be in the market for indiscriminate flings any more, it was satisfying to know she hadn't lost her touch.

In fact, as she took a long gulp of the watery diner coffee ten minutes later, she felt almost mellow. Until the revolving door at the front of the restaurant spun round and out popped Marnie Price looking cute and efficient in her power suit and kitten heels. Gina lifted a hand to wave, and watched Marnie's expression go from keen to wary when she spotted the empty seat next to her.

The hollow roll of regret flopped over in Gina's stomach. While it was certainly true that she and the Savannah Belle hadn't had a thing in common when they'd first met at Reese's house on campus—and Gina had spent most of that first month teasing Marnie mercilessly about everything from her views on love and marriage to her perfect Southern manners—their friendship had eventually developed into something strong and supportive and surprisingly genuine.

The truth was, Gina had felt superior to Marnie then. Gina had considered herself a sophisticated, cosmopolitan woman of the world who knew all she needed to know about men and sex and relationships—unlike the sheltered, self-confessed Southern virgin.

But Marnie had grown on Gina, despite their differences. Because beneath those pristine Southern manners had been an admirable devotion to doing the right thing, being accountable for your actions and always believing the best of people. And then Gina had gone and mucked everything up by jumping into bed with the brother Marnie idolised—and discovered in the process she was hardly the poster girl for mature relationships either.

But if there was something Gina regretted even more than giving in to temptation that night, it was taking that bright, trusting light out of Marnie's eyes. Something that now appeared to be gone for good.

'Hi, Gina.' Marnie sent her a polite smile as she slid into the booth. 'Are we early?' she asked, probably hoping Reese—who was never late—would magically materialise and get them out of this predicament.

If only. 'Reese can't make it. Something came up, apparently.' Gina took a judicious sip of her coffee, resisting the urge to say the something was probably a key part of the hot ex-husband's anatomy.

'And I'll bet I know what it is,' Marnie murmured, making Gina choke on her coffee. 'I swear, you'd think Mason had invented sex the way Reese gushes about the guy.'

Gina put down her cup, a grin forming despite the underlying tension. 'Gushes being the operative word.'

Marnie gave a small laugh. 'All I hope is that it's more than just sex this time around—because there is no way I am repackaging a billion truffles again in this lifetime.'

'Amen to that,' Gina said, toasting Marnie with her coffee mug and smiling at the memory of how the four of them had spent two solid hours taking table-top truffles out of engagement-ring-style boxes when Reese had decided to re-

invent her aborted wedding to Dylan into a celebration of...
Well, no one had ever really figured that out.

'To be frank,' Gina added, 'if I ever see another truffle
before I die, it'll be too soon.'

Marnie's lips curved, but Gina could see the concern in
her pure blue eyes—and had the sudden realisation that she
hadn't given Marnie her due in the last month.

Seemed they'd both done quite a lot of growing up in the
last decade.

After ordering herself an iced tea and some wheat toast
from the blushing waiter, Marnie got right down to business, tugging a smartphone out of her briefcase. 'Okay, I've
narrowed a couple of possible venues down that can accom-
modate a party of seven on the required date, can provide a
wedding cake and meet our "classy but not too intimidating"
requirements.' She pressed a few buttons, her gaze flicking
to Gina. 'My personal favourite is the Tribeca Terrace. Do
you know it?'

Gina nodded. 'Sure, chic and funky with sensational food
and a dance floor—so Cassie and Tuck can get up close and
pornographic for our benefit.'

Marnie's lips quirked again. 'It's pricey, but totally worth
it.'

'Done.'

Marnie blinked. 'What do you mean, done? We haven't
gone through the other options.... And don't you have any
venues you want to put forward?'

'I had a couple.' Gina shrugged. 'But none of them are
as perfect as the TriBee,' she said, giving it the nickname it
had acquired in the foodie press. 'You nailed it in one. Why
shop around?'

The waiter arrived with Marnie's toast and tea and made
a bit of a production about asking Gina if she had everything
she needed. As he left Gina noticed Marnie's gaze follow

him, before she concentrated on buttering her toast. There was no censure in the look, just a simple acknowledgement. But Gina could still hear the words running through Marnie's head even if the well-mannered woman would rather bite off her own tongue than voice them.

There goes another of Gina's conquests.

Ten years ago, Gina would have played up to that assessment and enjoyed it—and quite probably taken full advantage of whatever the young waiter had to offer. But not any more.

Placing her coffee mug back on the table, she waited for Marnie to stop buttering. When the bright blue eyes finally met hers, she could see the tension around the edges of Marnie's mouth and realised that—while she still had a low-grade urge to throttle Reese—their mutual friend had been right. They needed to get this out in the open, if they were going to have any chance of getting past it and repairing the friendship between the four of them the rest of the way.

Marnie and her would never be best friends, Gina had already screwed that up for good, but surely they could be more than just civil to each other. A bit more warmth between the two of them would also take the pressure off the other two—and as both Reese and Cassie had weddings coming up, she couldn't think of a better gift to give them both.

'I'm sure we both know why Reese didn't show this morning,' she said evenly. 'And for once I'm not convinced it has anything to do with her inability to leave Mason's bed first thing in the morning while he's still in it.'

Marnie's eyes widened a fraction. She raised her napkin to her mouth to remove an invisible crumb. 'Reese has always been a peace-maker.'

She put the napkin down, folded it carefully.

'But I'm confident she'll stop trying to be Mother Teresa when we turn up at Amber's Bridal tomorrow having booked

an awesome venue for Cassie's party without having gotten
into a catfight in the Grand Central Diner.'

Gina's lips curved at the droll statement. 'True, but funnily
enough…' She took a deep breath, fortified by the odd feeling of connection between them—because right about now
it seemed they both had a low-grade urge to throttle Reese.
'I think I can probably go one better than that.'

Wariness crossed Marnie's face. 'How?'

'By apologising for all the crappy things I said to you on
our last night together—which were cruel and juvenile and
totally unnecessary.' She huffed out a steady breath when
Marnie remained silent.

Now for the biggie.

'And more importantly by apologising for seducing your
brother the week beforehand—which was equally cruel and
juvenile and totally unnecessary.' Even if it had felt very necessary at the time.

'My only excuse is that I was in a bad place at the time.' A
bad place that had got a whole lot worse in the months after
that night. 'And I did bad things as a result—including being
a heartless, reckless, selfish, philandering tart. And although
I can't promise that I won't do bad things again—because if
there's one thing I despise more than a heartless tart, it's a
hypocrite—I'm trying a lot harder not to.'

Marnie's face remained unnervingly impassive, before she
gave her head a little nod. 'Thanks for the apology. But if you
were being cruel and juvenile, I was too. And…' She paused.
'While I could have done without such a graphic description
of my brother's…' she coughed, clearly struggling to get the
word out '…assets, you didn't say anything that wasn't true.'
She looked down at her hands, which were mangling the carefully folded napkin. 'Carter was the one that cheated, Gina.
Not you.' Her eyes met Gina's, disillusionment clouding the
blue depths. 'And after seeing his marriage die a slow, painful

death and seeing what a player he's become since his divorce—
I don't think you should take all the blame.'

A player? Carter?

Gina's throat constricted as the memories she'd filed
carefully away in the 'biggest disaster of my life' box had a
coming-out party.

Yes, he'd been devastatingly handsome, and moody and
magnetic and sexy enough to make any woman salivate un-
controllably, even an accomplished flirt like her. But beneath
that potent machismo had been a man who, like Marnie, had
been determined to do the right thing—who had been honourable and sensitive and touchingly reserved, despite the
hunger burning in those cool blue eyes. How could that man
be a player?

Nobody could change that much. Even in ten years....

'Reese told me Carter had got a divorce,' she said. The
guilt she'd worked hard to mask ever since Reese had told
her the news throbbed in her belly like a lump of radioactive
waste—alongside an inappropriate rush of heat, which she
studiously ignored.

'I'm sorry about that too,' she said. It would be conceited
of her to think she was wholly responsible for the failure of
Carter's marriage, but she still had to shoulder her share of
the blame. She'd slept with an engaged man and then tried
to push the blame onto the only innocent party in the whole
thing, Carter's fiancée, Missy.

'You don't need to apologise,' Marnie remarked with sober
certainty. 'The divorce wasn't your fault—they had a lot of
other...' her voice trailed off '...issues.'

'It's nice of you to say that.' And nicer still to see that she
actually meant it. 'But I was there when it happened, and I
know how hard he tried to resist me.'

Marnie shot her hands out in the shape of a T. 'All right,

time out, because you are straying back into "things I will never need to know about my brother" territory, here.'

Gina huffed out a laugh at the look of horror on Marnie's face. Maybe the Southern Belle had grown up, but it seemed she still had the same demure sensibilities when it came to discussing her big brother's sex life.

'The point is…' Marnie put her hands down '…I'm ashamed of the things I said that night too.' She drew a circle on the table. 'I wanted to put all the blame on you, because blaming Carter would mean admitting he didn't belong on the pedestal I'd put him on.' She sighed. 'We're not close these days.'

Gina felt the renewed stab of regret. 'Oh, Marnie, I'm so sorry. Did I do that too?'

'I don't think so,' Marnie said, sounding adamant. 'It would have happened anyway once I got older and wiser and realised what he was really like.' The wry smile on Marnie's lips did nothing to dispel the thoughtful expression. 'You know, I don't remember you having such an overdeveloped guilt complex.'

Gina chuckled at the observation. 'Unfortunately, it's the end result of believing everything is about you.'

Marnie sent her a quick grin, the unguarded moment a reminder of the easy friendship they'd once shared.

'Look, I hope we're good now,' Marnie said. 'Because my relationship with my brother isn't as important to me as my friendship with y'all.'

'Yeah, we're good,' Gina said, but felt oddly deflated as Marnie excused herself to go to the restroom.

Maybe they hadn't had a catfight, and maybe she'd finally got out the apology that she should have given Marnie ten years ago… But somehow it didn't feel like enough.

Maybe her thoughtless seduction that night hadn't been the only reason Carter's marriage had ended, but it had definitely helped to screw up his relationship with his sister. And Gina couldn't quite shake the thought that Marnie had fallen back on her perfect Southern manners to smooth everything over, but didn't really mean it.

The buzzing of Marnie's phone jolted Gina out of her guilt trip, and made coffee slosh over the rim of her mug. She mopped up the spill and made a grab for the phone as it vibrated towards the edge of the table. Then nearly dropped it at the photo that flashed up in the viewfinder under the text message.

Arrive @ The Standard 7pm 2nite. In NYC til next Fri. Txt me. We need 2 discuss yr allowance. C

Her heart leapt up to bump against her larynx and the swell of heat that she'd been busy ignoring flared. She pressed her thumb to the screen and ran it over the darkly handsome face that had hardly changed in ten years. His hair was longer, the brutal buzz cut now a mass of thick waves that curled around his ears and touched his collar. Those hollow cheeks had filled out a bit, the electric blue of his eyes looked colder and even more intense, and there were a few distinguished laughter lines, but otherwise Carter Price looked even hotter than she remembered him. She touched the tempting little dent in his chin—biting the tip of her tongue as a blast of memory assailed her. The rasp of stubble and the nutty taste of pistachio as she licked a rivulet of ice cream off his full bottom lip.

Stop fondling Marnie's phone, you muppet.

The sharp rap of metal on wood rang out as she dropped the phone on the table. Carter Price's unsettling gaze continued to stare at her, so she flipped it over—moments before Marnie appeared at her shoulder.

'Your phone was buzzing,' she offered, as nonchalantly

as she could manage, while blood coursed up her neck and pulsed at her temples.

'Right, thanks.' Marnie picked up the phone and slid back into the booth.

A frown formed on Marnie's forehead as she read the text. And Gina wondered for one agonising moment if Marnie would mention the texter—and then wondered how she was going to conduct a conversation while having a hot flush. But Marnie didn't say anything, she simply frowned, keyed in a few characters, pressed send and then tucked the phone into the pocket of the briefcase.

'Shall I go ahead and book the Tribeca Terrace?' she asked, her voice clear and steady and businesslike, the frown gone.

Gina's shoulders knotted with tension and the sinking feeling in her stomach dropped to her toes.

So Marnie had lied—maybe she wanted to pretend that they were both past what had happened ten years ago, that it didn't matter any more. But how could it be true when she couldn't even bring herself to mention Carter's name?

Marnie didn't trust her. And frankly who could blame her?

They made arrangements to meet up the next day for the bridesmaids' fittings at Reese's friend Amber's bridal boutique in the Manhattan Bridge Overpass District before Marnie—who seemed more than a little preoccupied—rushed off to get to her office in Brooklyn.

Gina watched her leave, and realised that there was only one way to win Marnie's trust—and prove to herself that she deserved it. And that was to finally make amends for everything that had happened ten years ago, on the night she'd thrown herself at a virtually married man.

She gulped down her lukewarm coffee as goosebumps prickled up her spine. Unfortunately that meant apologising to more than just Marnie.

CHAPTER TWO

GINA CLIMBED OUT of the cab under the High Line in New York's Meatpacking District and mounted the metal steps to the linear park constructed along an old L-train track. The concrete pathway, edged with planters of wild ferns and flowers, bustled with joggers, canoodling couples and families enjoying the pleasantly warm but not overly muggy New York evening.

Sweat trickled down her back as she stepped out of the heat into the cool lobby area of The Standard Hotel. The retro chic decor—all white plastic sculptures, distressed stone walls and dark leather scooped seats—made her feel as if she'd stepped onto the set of a sixties sci-fi movie.

She lifted her arms, to deter the sweat from dampening the armpits of the vintage Dior mini-dress she'd spent half an hour selecting from her extensive wardrobe of couture originals and thrift-store finds. The plan was to look cool and sophisticated and in control while finally confronting the ghosts of her past, not like a bedraggled rag doll.

She lingered for a moment—feeling a bit like an alien from the planet Zod—before taking a deep, calming breath, and stepping up to the reception desk.

The expertly coiffured receptionist took down the message she'd spent most of the afternoon composing. The perfect combination of polite, impersonal and not too pushy—the single sentence gave Carter the option of contacting her, so she could give him her apology in person.

Whether he would or not was entirely up to him. The sense of relief as she left the desk was immense. She'd done what she had to do. It really didn't matter now if Carter called her or not. But somehow she doubted he would.

Because as well as spending far too much time that afternoon composing the perfect message—she'd also spent rather a lot of it Googling information about the CEO of the Price Paper Consortium of Savannah, Georgia. After wasting a good twenty minutes poring over the numerous pictures, gossip items and local news reports featuring Carter Price and the ever-changing kaleidoscope of model-perfect 'possible future brides' who'd accompanied him to an array of high-society functions and charity events in the last few years, she'd had to concede that Marnie hadn't lied.

The sensitive, conflicted Southern gentleman who had once been so susceptible to her charms wasn't just a major player now, he appeared to be attempting a world record for dating and dumping the entire debutante population south of the Mason-Dixon Line.

This Carter was not the man who had rushed back to his childhood sweetheart crippled by guilt and self-loathing at what they had done. So she very much doubted he'd want to revisit that time in his life. But exactly how much of the change in him was her fault?

The thought struck and stopped her in her tracks—right beside the entrance to the hotel's lobby bar.

Damn, her throat felt as if she'd been swallowing sand. She glanced at her watch. Ten to six. Still an hour before Carter was due to check in. She had time for a soft drink without risking bumping into him.

She shrugged off the thought of how much Carter appeared to have changed in the last ten years as she entered the brightly lit bar. Apportioning blame for that now was a little late.

Crowded with New York's young and lively in-crowd celebrating the start of the weekend and a few tired-looking tourists ready to call it a day, the pristine blonde wooded space was already throbbing with life. One small table right on the outskirts of the action was still vacant. She nabbed it and waylaid a member of the wait staff.

'A club soda, please.... No, scratch that,' she said as indecision struck. 'Make that a small dry martini, light on the vermouth.' One drink couldn't hurt and she'd earned it.

When the martini arrived, Gina took a single sip, then placed it on the table in front of her, savouring the flowery taste of the gin and resisting the urge to down it in three quick gulps. She never drank to excess any more. Mostly because she now knew that inebriation had a direct correlation to stupid behaviour.

She speared the olive at the bottom of her glass with a cocktail stick and swirled it around, savouring the light buzz from the alcohol as the guttural chatter of the Japanese tourists at the next table cocooned her in the blessedly anonymous corner. The muggy scent of body odour and expensive perfumes and colognes overwhelmed the blast of cold air from the bar's air-conditioning system, drawing her back in time to a sultry summer afternoon a lifetime ago.

The ripples in her martini glass shimmered out to the rim and dissipated as the hazy memory floated at the edges of her consciousness and invaded her senses.

The phantom scent of lime polish and hyacinths tickled her nostrils as she recalled the pleasantly cool hallway of the clapboard house on Hillbrook College Campus. The parquet cold beneath bare feet as she tiptoed down the compact house's corridor with her shoes clutched in her fist. Guilt tugged at the pit of her stomach—because she was creeping home at four in the afternoon after an all-night frat party when she had promised faithfully to spend the day revising at the college library with Reese. And then she heard again the sound of an unfamiliar male voice, low and brusque despite being infused with the lazy rhythms of the Deep South, echoing down the stairs from Marnie's room on the first landing.

CHAPTER THREE

'No is my final answer, Marnie. Mama's not going to allow you to go on a road trip with your friends and neither am I. Once the wedding is over, you will be staying in Savannah for the summer.'

Gina's brows drew down in a sharp frown. So the famous older brother, the Sainted Carter, had finally showed up to transport Marnie's stuff back to Savannah. She slipped her shoes back on and decided to stay put in her hiding place—and get some vicarious pleasure from hearing Marnie give the guy the smack down he clearly deserved.

What a tool, ordering his sister about like that.

'I don't believe I need your permission, Carter,' Marnie replied, succinctly. 'You're not Daddy—and Mama will come around once I've spoken to her.'

Way to go, Marnie.

Pride swelled in Gina's chest at the knowledge that a year ago, when Marnie had first arrived at Reese's house on campus from deepest, darkest Georgia, she never would have had the guts to talk back to the Sainted Carter like that. A man Gina and Reese and Cassie had all suspected was a total douche, hence the nickname they'd given him together, despite the way Marnie gushed about him.

'Mama doesn't control the mill's finances, I do,' came the

low, irritatingly patient reply. 'So I'd like to know how you're gonna go on this road trip, if I refuse to pay for it.'

'Daddy left me a share in the mill, surely I can—'

'Daddy left your share in trust,' he interrupted with the same implacable calm. 'A trust which he left me to administer until you reach your majority—and I'm refusing your request for funds on this occasion.'

'That's not fair, Carter.'

Gina's fingers fisted into tight balls as the argument continued and slowly but surely all the confidence and assurance Marnie had gained in the past year leached away as her brother refused to budge. In fact, Gina was fairly sure from his uninterested replies that he wasn't even listening.

For that alone, Gina could have throttled him with her bare hands. Why did so many men have to be like her father, judgmental and superior and always, always right?

She pressed back into the alcove as Marnie's bedroom door closed upstairs and footsteps came down the stairs. She caught a glimpse of a tall figure dressed in a creased chambray shirt and suit trousers as he strolled into the kitchen.

She stayed in the alcove, hearing his heavy sigh, and debated the wisdom of getting involved: with her tendency to be provocative she was liable to make it worse, and it really wasn't any of her business. But as she walked to the kitchen doorway and spied on him helping himself to one of Reese's chilled diet colas from the fridge, anger and resentment flared.

He closed the fridge, his broad back to her as he twisted the cap off the bottle and flipped it into the bin, then took a long swallow of the cola. One large hand gripped the edge of the sink but the rigid line of his shoulder blades relaxed.

Why should she respect his privacy when he hadn't respected Marnie's—and how could she possibly make things worse?

Leaning insolently against the doorjamb, she gave her voice the soft smoky purr she knew made men putty in her hands. 'You know, you really ought to take that huge stick out from up your arse. It's going to ruin the very nice line of those designer trousers.'

He swung round and her lungs seized in astonishment.

It seemed Marnie had failed to mention one fairly crucial bit of information about her big brother during all the gushing this year. Carter Price was a total hottie.

At six foot two or three, with mile-wide shoulders and the tanned skin of a pirate, he was as big and dark as his sister was small and fair, but the relationship was confirmed by the striking eyes that narrowed on her face—and shared the exact same shade of cerulean blue as his sister's. On Marnie they looked cute and appealing. On her brother they looked cold and intense.

The unblinking gaze drifted down her frame as he took another swig of the stolen cola and Gina felt the prickle of response, everywhere.

She settled back against the doorjamb, but clamped down on the urge to stretch her back—thus displaying what she knew to be an exceptional pair of breasts to their best advantage.

Focus, Gina. You're not here to flirt with the guy. You're here to tell him a thing or two about women's emancipation— and his sister's emancipation in particular.

'You've got quite a mouth on you, miz.' The deep drawl was as slow and seductive as molasses but for the steely hint of censure beneath. 'My daddy would have taken a hickory switch to my backside if I'd used that sort of language in the presence of a lady.'

'I guess we're both very fortunate then that you're not in the presence of a lady,' she replied tartly.

Carter Price wasn't just a hottie, he was also a sexist control freak, but no way was he going to control her, with his cool Southern manners and his total contempt for a women's right to self-determination.

She let her gaze drift over him too. 'Because I'd really hate to see what I can imagine is an exceptionally cute backside being whipped with a hickory switch—unless I was the one doing it.'

Let's see how you like being objectified, Buster.

Two dark eyebrows arched, and she felt the wave of satisfaction at the knowledge that she'd shocked him. Gina Carrington was no simpering Southern miss prepared to bow down to the dictates of a man. And the sooner Carter Price got that message, the better. But then his irises darkened and his lips twitched at the edges. And she had the strangest feeling she might have underestimated him, a tad.

'Why do I get the feeling your daddy didn't take a hickory switch to…' he paused to direct his gaze pointedly at her mid-section and she had to resist the urge to tuck in her bottom '…what I can see is also an exceptionally cute butt, nearly often enough?'

She wanted to be outraged at the suggestion—and any mention of her father and/or the corporal punishment of a child would ordinarily do that—but unfortunately she wasn't outraged. Because she was far too distracted by the surge of heat making her nipples tighten against the confines of her bra and the way her cute *butt* was now sizzling alarmingly.

'You're very perceptive, Mr Price. My father never hit me,' she informed him with as much dignity as she could muster while her behind was still pulsing from the imagined thrashing. 'Because he knew he would lose an arm if he tried,' she finished, with the purr still firmly in place, even though it was starting to sound less and less like an affectation—and more and more like an invitation.

'Seems to me an arm is a small price to pay when it comes to instilling good manners in your child.'

The outrage came without a problem this time as the sizzle fizzled out. The man was serious.

'If you actually believe that hitting a child—or a woman—is less heinous than bad manners, then an arm isn't the only thing you deserve to lose.'

She could see she'd done a lot more than shock him this time, when he stiffened and the twitch on those firm sensual lips disappeared. 'You mistake me, miz?'

'Carrington. Gina Carrington.'

'Miz Carrington. I've never hit a child, or a woman, in my life, and I never would. I respect women. Absolutely.'

'Is that something else your daddy taught you with his hickory switch?' she said, the contempt dripping now.

But instead of the smug affirmative she had expected, something flickered across his face, and she had the feeling she'd crossed a line she hadn't intended to. He turned away, and braced one hand against the sink. Then fixed her with an unsettling stare. 'You seem to have a problem with me, Miz Carrington. And as this is the first time I've had the pleasure of your company, I'd like to know why!'

It occurred to her that he hadn't answered her question, but this was the opening she'd been waiting for, so she took it.

'I heard you upstairs, bullying Marnie into doing what you wanted. Not what she wanted. She's eighteen years old and perfectly capable of coming on a road trip with us this summer. And as I understand it, you'll be on your honeymoon anyway, so why is it so important to have her sitting in Savannah twiddling her thumbs instead of having fun with us?'

The grim line of his lips thinned out and a muscle in his jaw clenched. 'So your exemplary manners include eavesdropping?'

'It would seem so.' What did she care what some self-

righteous Southern prig thought of her manners? 'And while
we're on the subject, there happens to be several things in life
that are a great deal more important than exemplary manners.
And letting your sister follow her heart's desire happens to
be one of them.'

'Going on a road trip with y'all hasn't got a damn thing to
do with following her heart's desire.'

So much for his Southern manners, Gina thought, rel-
ishing the spurt of temper. At last, here was something she
could work with; she happened to be very good at handling
male tantrums.

'How would you know that?' she said coolly.

'Because she's my sister.'

'And that makes you her keeper, does it? Perhaps Marnie
doesn't need a keeper any more.'

His brows furrowed into a deep frown and she could
almost see the frustration pumping off him. She knew he
wanted to say something derogatory about her, and Reese
and possibly Cassie right about now.

Because what other reason could he have for wanting to
keep his sister away from them?

She waited for him to accuse all three of them of being a
bad influence, but to her surprise, after several deep breaths,
his shoulders relaxed and she saw him visibly draw himself
back from the brink.

She dismissed the moment of admiration—control after
all wasn't one of her strong points.

'I don't consider myself to be Marnie's keeper, Miz Carrington,' he said, in a tight voice, the drawl no longer quite so
pronounced. 'But I am her brother and I intend to do what's
best for her—with or without your consent.'

Her lips curved in a wry smile. Talk about getting hoisted
by your own petard. It seemed Carter's perfect manners were
going to prevent him from saying what he actually thought

about her and her friends. Well, she hoped swallowing that down gave him heartburn. 'And why is what's best for her your decision and not hers?'

The muscle in his jaw pulsed. 'Because she's eighteen,' he said. But she could see what he wasn't saying in that look of calm condescension. *And because she's a woman.*

'How old are you, Carter?' she asked.

The frown deepened, as if he were looking for the trap. 'I'm twenty-two.'

'And how old were you when you got engaged?' she asked, although she already knew the answer, because Marnie had talked about her big brother's insanely romantic engagement to her best friend, Missy, incessantly when she'd first arrived at the house.

'It's not the same thing,' he said, seeing the trap too late.

'Umm-hmm. And why ever not? You were the same age as Marnie is now and yet you were mature enough to decide you were going to love your childhood sweetheart for the rest of your life.' She said the words with conviction, but couldn't help feeling a little sick to her stomach.

When had she ever been that romantic? That naïve? To believe that anyone was worth that much of a commitment?

'It wasn't like that. Missy and I are well suited. And it was the right thing to do after my father died. My mother and Marnie needed stability and they were both in favour of the match.'

It was Gina's turn to frown. And not just because Carter's description of the engagement was in sharp contrast to the wildly romantic whirlwind of love and devotion Marnie had described. Who the hell proposed marriage because they were being sensible? And he'd made it sound as if the primary motivation had been the approval of his mother and his kid sister? She was by no means a hopeless romantic, but wasn't that taking filial duty a bit too far?

'But you do love Missy, right?' The question popped out before she could stop it.

He looked taken aback. As well he might, because this really was none of her business. But curiosity consumed her. He'd only been eighteen. What on earth had he been thinking settling for 'The One' so young? What about hormones? And exploring your options? And sowing wild oats?

'Of course I love Missy. She's going to be my wife in two weeks' time. We're friends, we understand each other and we both want the same things out of life.'

None of which sounded remotely like convincing reasons for proposing marriage when you were just out of high school. But what did she know? 'What things?'

He shrugged, the movement stiff and defensive. And she realised for the first time that he looked unsure of himself. 'Companionship, trust, compatibility, children. Eventually.' The affirmation came out in a monotone, as if he'd rehearsed it a hundred times.

'Why, Rhett,' Gina said, fluttering her eyelashes and affecting a simpering Southern drawl. 'I can see how you must have swept Missy off her feet with that proposal. How romantic of you to compile a checklist for the perfect marriage.'

'Missy knows she can trust me,' he said firmly, the look on his face delightfully annoyed and confused. Clearly the Sainted Carter wasn't used to being teased—or questioned about his carefully planned love life. 'That's what matters.'

'Really? What about love and passion and adventure and...' she groped for another quality that might get the message across to this indomitable and resolutely anti-romantic man '...and the promise of multi-orgasmic sex for the rest of your life?'

His gaze flicked to her cleavage, then shot back to her face and a dull shade of red rose up his neck and made his tan glow on chiselled cheekbones. He looked away, taking a large fortifying gulp of the cola. And suddenly she knew.

Oh. My. God.

Carter Price had been eighteen when he'd proposed to his very-appropriate fiancée. And if Missy was as much of a sanctimonious prude as her best friend, Marnie, had been when she'd first arrived from Savannah—wearing a little promise ring on her finger that signified her purity, and had needled Gina no end—then Missy had probably demanded she remain a virgin until her wedding night.

She searched the long tanned fingers of Carter's left hand wrapped around the cola bottle. Was it possible that Carter had made a similar promise? Hadn't Marnie said boys wore them too, when Gina had lit into her for being a disgrace to Women's Liberation. Gina held back the gasp as she spotted the silver band on Carter's pinkie, identical to the celibacy ring that Marnie no longer wore when she was at college.

Oh, no, surely not? A man who was as virile and handsome and overwhelmingly male as he was, and who looked at her with that dark sexual intensity he couldn't hide? That man hadn't had sex since he was eighteen? It was just too delicious. And too ridiculous. No wonder he looked so tense and uptight. And no wonder he was far too involved in Marnie's personal life, because he clearly didn't have one of his own.

An intervention was called for.

The surge of excitement and anticipation gripped Gina's chest—and some other interesting parts of her anatomy. Suddenly she had the perfect way to bring the Sainted Carter down a peg or two. Prove to him that he was as human and fallible and sinful as the rest of them.

She was after all an accomplished flirt. And there was no harm in simply flirting with the man. Especially a man as stuffy and controlling and undeniably hot as this one. And once she'd proved to Carter Price that bad girls were people

too, once she'd reduced him to a puddle of overactive hormones and sexual desperation, she'd be able to get him to
agree to anything.... Even letting his innocent kid sister go
on a riotous road trip with three loose women.

The man was celibate. He hadn't had sex in four long years.
The challenge was simply irresistible. She'd lost her virginity at sixteen with her thirty-five-year-old biology teacher
at St Bude's boarding school, and she hadn't looked back
since. Carter Price wouldn't know what hit him. And while
she wouldn't do the dirty deed with him, because she never
poached on another woman's territory, why shouldn't she take
her flirtation far enough to get Saint Carter primed and ready
for his wedding night? Missy would end up thanking her.

'Would you like another martini, miss?'

Gina blinked, staring absently at the harassed young waitress as the question brought her spinning back to the present.
And the bar at The Standard where she'd gone for a quick fortifying libation. And been blind-sided by too many memories.

She looked down at her glass, surprised to find it empty,
the olive on its cocktail stick lined up on the table. 'No,
thanks, just the check, please.'

The waitress nodded, clearing away the empty glass.

Tension tightened Gina's stomach as the reality of exactly
how reckless and manipulative she'd been that night slammed
into her in all its grim glory.

Maybe Marnie was right, and Carter was the one who had
been cheating.

But there was no getting away from the fact that she had
seduced him. Not the other way around. And it wasn't until
twelve hours after meeting him in the kitchen and making a
conscious decision to bend him to her will that she'd finally
been forced to admit the magnitude of her mistake. As she lay
in the dew-drenched grass under a maple tree, the dawn light

casting a redolent glow on the rebel wave in Carter's cropped hair, her heart beating a staccato rhythm of shock and guilt, her thighs spread and aching, his erection still huge inside her and his pinkie ring cutting into her cheek.

Heat washed through her at the visceral memory—and it occurred to Gina that maybe the decision to cab it over to the High Line this evening and deliver her carefully composed message in person, when she could just as easily have phoned or emailed it, might have a lot more significance than she wanted to admit.

Had she on some subconscious level hoped to bump into the man whose picture she'd glimpsed on Marnie's smartphone that morning—for reasons other than closure and accountability? Was her new leaf not as well turned over as she thought?

Crap! She needed to get out of here now.

The waitress returned with the check, and Gina threw several bills on the tray without counting them. The guilty flush made her breathing speed up as she shot across the lobby.

Gloria Gaynor singing 'I Will Survive' blasted from her bag at top volume, making her steps falter. It took her a moment to remember that Gloria's strident disco classic was her phone's ringtone.

She paused, fumbled for the phone and stared at a number she didn't recognise. Glancing at the clock above the lobby's exit doors, she felt a little of the panic retreat. She still had thirty minutes before Carter was due to arrive. She took a steadying breath and clicked the answer button. This might be a new client responding to her recent social media campaign for new business. She couldn't afford not to answer. She'd simply have to talk and run.

But as she pressed the phone to her ear the deep laconic Southern accent had the heels of her sandals sinking into the deep pile purple carpet and her heart pounding into her throat.

'Hello, Gina. It's Carter Price. I got your message.'

'Carter. Hi. How are you?' she said, the false brightness making her wince.

Good grief, was he at the reception desk? Right behind her? Maybe he'd phoned ahead? Please let him have phoned ahead. She couldn't risk turning around to check. So she kept walking. The exit doors were only a few feet away.

'I'm good,' came the husky reply. 'Although I'm wondering where you're off to in such a hurry.'

Crapola!

She spun round. The phone dropping away from her ear as she spotted the man standing less than ten feet away, with one elbow propped against the reception desk, a phone at his ear—and cool aquamarine eyes locked on her face.

Her breath got trapped somewhere around her solar plexus—as she debated the probability of teleportation actually existing.

Beam me up, Scottie. Right now.

'Don't move,' he said into his phone, before switching it off and tucking it into his back pocket.

Her thighs quivered alarmingly as he walked towards her. She locked her knees, determined not to collapse into a heap as the shot of adrenaline collided with the explosion of heat in the pit of her stomach—and it occurred to her that the paparazzi pictures had not done him justice. Savannah's most eligible bachelor wasn't just hot, he was positively combustible.

She forced air through her burning lungs, grateful for the fortifying buzz from her martini as he got close enough for her to pick up the smell of soap and man—and remember how much taller he was. At five foot seven, she wasn't used to men towering over her, but Carter Price had no trouble at all making her feel like a midget.

His steady gaze swept over her—then arrived back at her face. 'It's been a while, Miz Carrington.'

But not nearly long enough, if the sweat popping up on her top lip was anything to go by.

'You've improved with age,' he said, his tone low and amused. 'Like a fine wine.'

So had he, she thought. The few strands of grey at his temples, the new creases round his mouth, the crinkles at the corners of his eyes and the waves of thick dark hair that now touched the collar of his white shirt only adding to the confident, take-charge charisma that had been all too evident in the paparazzi pictures.

Say something, you silly cow!

'It's flattering of you to say so,' she murmured, struggling to maintain cool distance and not give in to the throaty purr.

His gaze strayed to her cleavage and her breathing quickened again, keeping a natural rhythm with the pounding beat of her pulse. But then the heavily lidded gaze met hers. The deep, lazy Southern accent reverberated across her nerve-endings. 'It's good to see you again. Marnie told me you were living in New York now,' he said, surprising her.

So he had asked Marnie about her. And Marnie had answered.

Then, to her utter astonishment, he took her hand in long, cool fingers and lifted it to his lips. The quick gallant buzz on her knuckles spun her back in time to the clean-cut young man he'd once been. But then his thick dark lashes caught the overhead light as he blinked slowly, and the inscrutable gaze had all thoughts of the boy disappearing—until all she could see was the man.

'How about we catch up in the bar? And you can tell me what's on your mind?'

'Okay, that would work,' she said, thinking no such thing. His hand settled on the small of her back as he directed her towards the bar.

Terrific! How the heck was she going to get her head round the perfectly simple apology she'd planned, while her mind was being fried to a crisp by all the zaps of electrical energy now radiating up her spine?

CHAPTER FOUR

CARTER PRICE BLINKED eyes gritty from jet lag after his flight from Russia that afternoon, the fog in his brain blown off course by the pulse of heat in his gut.

After ten years of denial, the two-line message the receptionist had handed him had confused him—and shaken him a little. More than a little if he was being entirely honest. He'd thought about Gina Carrington way too much over the years. So the sight of her dashing towards the exit doors had an effect on his senses somewhere in the region of a category five hurricane.

She looked hotter than he remembered her. And he remembered a lot. The beestung lips, the wide green, slightly slanting eyes, the mass of chestnut hair that had tumbled over her shoulders in riotous curls back then, but was now piled on top of her head, making his fingers itch to send it tumbling again. Her tall, slender figure had filled out some since her college days—her high breasts were fuller, her hips more generous, and her legs looked never-ending in the ice-pick heels. The overall effect made all those lush curves even more mouth-watering.

He'd dated a lot of women since popping his cherry with Gina Carrington, and divorcing his wife, most of them a lot more conventionally beautiful—but not one of them oozed pure, unadulterated sex the way Gina did. Or sent a right hook to his senses with a single whiff of their spicy, sultry scent.

He shook off the thought as she perched on a bar stool.

Get your mind out of your pants.

Boy, did he need ten hours straight—he really had to be losing it if he was fantasising about the woman who had once blown his life to smithereens.

Not that he blamed her for that. He'd been like a fire-cracker, waiting to explode. All she'd done was light the fuse.

He caught the barman's attention. 'What'll it be?' he asked Gina.

'Club soda.'

'Make mine a Sam Adams,' he added, propping himself on the stool beside her.

He watched her throat bob as she swallowed heavily—and felt the surge of satisfaction. She seemed a little jumpy—and she'd definitely been planning to run out on him. Which gave him the upper hand. He made a habit now of never being at a disadvantage with women—and that went double for this woman, because she'd once had him at the biggest disad-vantage of all.

But there had been a whole lot of water under the bridge, not to mention ladies in his bed, since that night. And he wasn't that lust-driven sex-deprived delusional kid any more. His pulse spiked as she pursed her full lips around the straw in her club soda and sucked.

He took a sip of the yeasty micro-beer.

Relax.

So what if he had some lingering lust issues where Gina Carrington was concerned? He had the control not to act on them now. Or at least not straight away. Not until he knew the score. His gaze skimmed over the silky dress and noticed how her magnificent rack rose and fell in staggered rhythm against the snug bodice.

Yeah, definitely edgy. A gratifying change from their first meeting, when she'd had all the moves and he'd been the one playing catch-up.

He took a long draft of his beer and waited for her to speak. She'd been the one to contact him, after all.

She glugged down a good portion of the soda, getting more jumpy by the second, but didn't elaborate, so he decided to push it. Her note hadn't exactly given much away. 'So I hear you've got your own business—website development and social-media strategy, right?'

Her eyes darted to his, the wary look gratifying. 'How do you know that?'

He shrugged. 'I've been thinking of investing in a social-media strategist for the mill. Your name came up in the research we did.'

And after the shock of seeing her name on the report, he'd looked her up on the Internet and discovered she was now living in the U.S. Not that he planned to tell her that.

Once he and Missy had called it quits, he'd been able to let go of the guilt over his night with Gina, and how much it had snuck into his dreams during the years of his marriage.

Given his current reaction to Gina, it was clear guilt wasn't the problem any more.

'Nice site, by the way,' he added. 'Clean and clear, and you've got some great testimonials there.'

'Thank you.' She watched him intently and he noticed the beguiling flecks of gold in the green of her irises.

'Is that why you contacted me?' He pushed some more.

Her eyebrows launched up her forehead. 'God, no! I'm not that desperate for new business.'

He grinned at her outraged denial, surprised to realise he was glad she hadn't gotten in touch just to tout for business. She took another long sip of the soda, but didn't say anything else. 'Then you're gonna have to give me a hint—because your message was kind of cryptic.'

She let out a puff of breath. 'Right.' She faced him, her long legs crossed at the knees and her short dress riding up to display a distracting amount of toned, lightly tanned thigh.

'I was having coffee with Marnie this morning and saw your text message,' she began. 'When I discovered you were going to be in town for the week, I decided to take the opportunity to…' She hesitated. 'To come here and apologise for what I did to you ten years ago.' The last bit came out in a rush as if she'd had to push the words out.

The heat kicked harder in his gut. She looked totally sincere. Was she actually serious? And what the hell had brought this on, ten years after the event?

'You're gonna have to be a lot more specific,' he said, exhilarated when her eyes flashed with annoyance. It felt good to have this particular woman at this much of a disadvantage. 'Because as I recall we did a lot of things that night.'

Gina's temper simmered at the wry comment. Was he making fun of her? And if so why? The failure of his marriage was hardly a joking matter, surely?

'I'm apologising for all of it,' she said, more sharply than she had intended when his lips twisted with amusement. 'For seducing you, and taking your virginity and ruining your marriage.'

The glass he'd been lifting to his lips hit the bar with a snap as his brows shot towards his hairline. 'You have got to be kidding me?' A choked chuckle burst out.

'Actually I'm not.' The retort did nothing to cut through the rumble of incredulous laughter. 'I'm sincerely sorry for what I did to you.'

Heat spread across her chest as he continued to chuckle. She lifted her purse off the bar, slid off her stool, the sincerity of her apology drowning in a puddle of humiliation. She'd made a twit of herself; time to make a dignified exit. 'I should go. Thanks for the drink, Carter.'

But as she went to walk past him strong fingers snagged her wrist. 'Where are you off to in such a hurry?'

'I'm leaving. Obviously this was a mistake.' She twisted her arm; his fingers tightened.

'Not a chance, sugar.' The casual endearment became *shoo gah* in his low Southern drawl—and sounded so ridiculously sensuous she lost the will to resist for a moment.

He took the opportunity to place both palms on her waist and drew her towards him. She tensed, her will returning in a rush when she found herself positioned between his spread thighs. 'What are you doing?'

'Settle down, Gina. You wanted to talk, now it's my turn.'

She lifted her arms, in an attempt to step free without making too much of a scene, but his grip remained firm, anchoring her to the spot.

'Relax,' he said, still sounding amused. 'You're not going anywhere until I get to say what I wanna say.'

'Fine.' She folded her arms across her chest, disturbed by the long slow pull of arousal as his large hands drifted down to bracket her hips. 'You have my undivided attention. But I'm not sure what else there is to say.'

'That's because you've had your say.' He had the cheek to chuckle again. 'Now you get to listen.'

'Okay then, speak,' she snapped. They did not need to be standing this close, but short of putting on a show for the rest of the bar's inhabitants, who were already taking more of an interest in their conversation than she would have liked, she didn't appear to have much of a choice.

'I can see you're as quick-tempered as you ever were.'

She sent him a bland look. 'Is that what you wanted to say?'

He barked out another laugh. 'Point taken. I'll get on with
it. I sure wouldn't want to bore you.'

One muscled thigh touched her hip and she shifted away
from it, only to get trapped against the other one. Bored
wasn't the word that was first and foremost in her mind at
the minute.

'First off, you can shove your apology in one of those sweet
places where the sun doesn't shine.'

She sucked in a breath, shocked by his crudity. 'That's
nice, I must—'

'Hush, I'm still talking here.'

She shut her mouth.

Well, really. What had happened to those genteel manners?

'Second of all. You might have been my first, but I wasn't
that much of a sap. You didn't take me, I took you.'

Heat cascaded through her at the seductive growl, which
made her even more aware of the muscled thigh pressing
against her hip.

'And thirdly, I screwed up my marriage all on my own,
with no help from you.'

'I fail to see how you can say that, when I seduced you
two weeks before your wedding day,' she argued, getting a
little miffed at the lecturing tone. Where did he get off talking to her as if she were a two-year-old? 'I knew you were
engaged and yet I set out to seduce you, deliberately, without
a thought to your fiancée or anything else.'

'I believe I already covered that in point two,' he remarked,
his eyes brightening with amusement—which only caused
her temper to sizzle alongside the heat. 'You didn't force me
to do a damn thing I didn't want to do. So you can quit getting your panties in a twist ten years after the fact.'

'Oh, pur-lease,' she hissed, struggling to keep the decibel
level down in the face of his stubbornness. 'Just because you
now want to look at that night through testosterone-tinted

glasses it doesn't alter the fact that I put the moves on you, not the other way around. For goodness' sake, I had to practically throw myself at you before you'd even so much as kiss me.'

'So I was a slow starter. So what? I got the message eventually.'

'I know you did, that's not what I was trying to—'

His hands rode up to her waist, cutting off her protest in mid-sentence.

'Excuse me? Do you mind?' she yelped as those piercing blue eyes went from dark to dangerous and he leant forward to sniff at her hair.

'Not at all.'

She shifted back, but he only grinned, obviously enjoying her skittishness.

'You smell different,' he murmured. 'Did you change your shampoo?'

'In ten years?' she said, disarmed by the perceptive enquiry. 'Yes, of course.'

'I like it. More sophisticated but still sexy as sin.'

'Right.' She eased back, the pulse of arousal getting out of control. 'I really have to go.'

His hands dropped, but then he reached up to tuck a strand of hair behind her ear. 'No, you don't.' He patted the stool she had vacated. 'Stick around. One more drink. Let's talk. We never did get much of a chance to do that ten years ago.'

She should say no. Sitting next to him and sharing a companionable drink was a dangerous game to play while her erogenous zones were in meltdown. But when he shifted, his hand pressing into her waist to direct her to the stool next to him, and whispered: 'What's the matter, sugar? Scared you won't be able to resist seducing me again?' the tension snapped inside her and she laughed.

The statement should have sounded impossibly arrogant, but with that wicked light dancing in his eyes it sounded more like a challenge. And she'd never been able to resist one of those.

She gave him a deliberate once over, allowing her gaze to linger on the broad muscles of his chest and the sprinkle of chest hair revealed in the open neck of his shirt. 'I'm sure I can manage if I put my mind to it.'

He let out a rough chuckle. 'Touché.' He sat back on his stool. 'Take a seat. You know you want to.'

While she was sorely tempted to call him on the arrogant assumption, unfortunately she couldn't, quite. Because he was right. She did want to stay—and not just because of the potent arousal pulsing through every pore. She wanted to know why and how he'd changed so much—because the relaxed, charming, sexually confident hottie in front of her was nothing like the earnest and extremely uptight hottie she remembered.

'Okay, you've got me,' she said, conceding. 'One more club soda for the road.' She hopped back onto the stool beside him.

'Only a soda? It's Friday night? You didn't become a good girl when I wasn't looking, did you?'

'Hardly.' She snorted out another laugh at the wry comment. 'I've simply discovered that alcohol adds pounds where it's exceptionally hard to take them off again. And half an hour in the gym every morning is mind-numbingly boring enough.' And she had a feeling that keeping her wits about her in the next twenty minutes or so while they had their one drink for old times' sake was going to be fairly important.

His lips curved, shooting her blood pressure up a notch. *Make that very important.*

His gaze drifted down her figure, making her nipples tighten and her thigh muscles loosen. 'It sure appears to be time well spent.'

Make that completely imperative.

'I'll let my personal trainer know,' she quipped, fidgeting

with the straw of her dead soda—and ruthlessly stifling the wave of warmth. 'I'm sure she'll appreciate the compliment.'

'You do that,' he murmured before turning to signal the barman.

The sleeve of his shirt stretched across his biceps as he did so, drawing her gaze, and the wave of warmth crested. She tore her eyes away from the bulge of muscle flexing under the white linen and cleared her throat.

You can survive one more drink with the guy, surely.

She'd turned over a new leaf in the years since she'd jumped Carter Price at Hillbrook College and kick-started a chain of events that had changed both their lives irrevocably... But one drink was all she planned to risk.

If only she could have kept that resolve front and centre. And she probably would have, if he'd carried on flirting with her so openly—because she happened to be an expert at verbal foreplay. But it turned out the new Carter was a whole lot craftier than she'd given him credit for.

One drink turned into two and then three, until she stopped counting, as the man captivated her—not so much with those damn biceps, or the openly hungry looks, but with his knowledge and enthusiasm, when she steered the conversation to what she had thought would be the neutral topic of their working lives.

He talked with an infectious pride and dispassionate insight into the challenges he'd faced and overcome to drag the paper mill he'd inherited from his father when he was only seventeen into a thriving business. Then he'd listened with interest—and a surprising lack of criticism—to the string of careers she'd tried out before starting her web-design business last year.

They'd touched on a few personal topics—such as the hellish heat in Savannah in August, and her move from Lon-

don to New York five years ago—but had neatly sidestepped
anything too personal such as his marriage or his sister, or
the apology that she'd originally come to deliver. Until, after
two solid hours of non-stop conversation, Carter Price had
managed to lull her into a sense of security.

Unfortunately, during their very grown-up, surprisingly
comfortable conversation, she'd found herself becoming more
and more aware of him on a purely physical level: the low
appreciative rumble of his laughter that made the skin on
her spine tingle; the flash of interest in his eyes that made
her voice slip instinctively into the smoky purr of her youth;
the intense expression when he was outlining the different
funding options she might want to explore for her business,
which reminded her of the expression he'd once worn when
exploring her.

The hotel bar was emptying out, as New York's Friday
night party people headed out to pastures new, and the sub-
dued lighting, the intimate silences only made her more and
more aware of the desire to make the conversation just a
teensy weensy bit less comfortable. Now that he was an ur-
bane, successful and well-travelled businessman instead of
the sheltered boy he'd once been, what would be the harm in
spicing things up a little?

After all, given the recent pressures of work, and the emotional stress of trying to repair the damage she'd done to the
Awesome Foursome, she'd had a rather difficult summer so
far. Flirting in particular had been off the agenda—especially
flirting with someone as delicious as Carter Price.

'So, Carter, there is one thing I'd really love to know…'
She stabbed her straw into the Cosmopolitan he'd insisted
on ordering her after too many club sodas. 'For a man who's
so dedicated to his business,' she continued, not quite able
to resist a small purr when she took a sip of the Cosmo and
his gaze dipped to her mouth, 'and has clearly spent a great

deal of time and effort making it successful, I'd really love to know how you find enough spare time to date and dump so many different women.'

His brows winged up and then he chuckled—the easy sound triggering a new wave of tingles up her spine. 'Why, Gina, have you been checking up on me?'

She savoured another sip of the heady citrus-flavoured cocktail—not caring in the slightest that she'd been busted. 'I'll admit, I indulged in a quick Google this afternoon purely out of curiosity, you understand.'

'Oh, yeah,' he said, his voice lowering deliciously. 'I understand entirely.'

'And frankly I was quite staggered by the profligacy of your dating habits.'

'The profligacy, huh?' His lips curved, making her heart rate spike deliciously. 'I love when you use those longs words—they match that snooty English accent so well.'

'Flattery will get you nowhere. Answer the question.'

'There was a question in there?' he asked, the mock innocence making her grin back at him.

'You know very well there was—about your profligacy and your time-management skills,' she prompted. 'Which appear to be phenomenal if the evidence I found on the Internet is anything to go by. I did a little survey actually. And counted four different dates on your arm since you took Anjelique Montclair to the Georgia Governor's Ball on New Year's Eve.' She huffed to illustrate the point. 'I have major frock envy over that fabulous dress she had on, by the way. Very classy.' Not to mention a tiny bit of envy over how delicious Anjelique's date had looked in his tuxedo.

'She did look good, if I recall correctly,' he mused, still not answering the question, and not looking abashed in the slightest by her observation. Then again, she hadn't really expected him to.

'So?' she prompted again, actually more curious than she wanted to admit. 'Where *do* you find the time? Not to mention the stamina?'

He watched her, his gaze taking on a challenging glow, and the reckless thrill made her pulse leap.

Game on.

'The time and the stamina's easy to find, because while I'm socialising I'm usually working as well. Anjelique's father is a close friend of the governor's and I wanted an introduction to expedite a zoning request that the city council had been sitting on for months.' The smile he sent her was smug and completely unrepentant. 'In the South, mixing business with pleasure is the only way to get things done.'

'That sounds exhausting,' she said—and remarkably cynical. Had Anjelique realised he was dating her to expedite a zoning request?

'Not necessarily,' he murmured, his voice husky.

'How so?'

'Because I don't sleep with every woman I date.'

'Ah, I see.' She felt her cheeks heat. She hadn't expected him to be quite that blunt. Or for the admission to please her quite so much. But she quashed the burning desire to ask him directly if he'd slept with Anjelique. 'That's a relief.'

'It is?' he asked, lifting her hand from the bar to toy with her fingers. 'Why is that?'

The heat shot straight up her arm and joined the tingles migrating up her spine.

She tugged her fingers out of his. Damn, she'd walked right into that one. She certainly didn't want him thinking she was *that* interested in his love life. 'Because sleeping with someone to expedite a zoning request doesn't seem terribly romantic,' she remarked, struggling for flippant while her knickers were dampening with need.

'Uh-huh. When did you start thinking sex has anything to do with romance?'

When I slept with you.

She erased the foolish thought, and the silly spurt of vulnerability that came with it, and dipped her head to peer into her half-finished Cosmo.

Where had that come from? It wasn't even true—their night together had been hot and reckless and exhilarating, but ultimately wrong. Proving that even she had the capacity to confuse sex with romance. She pushed the drink away. Especially when she'd had too much to drink.

'I don't,' she replied, ignoring the blip in her heart rate at the intense watchfulness in his gaze. 'But maybe Anjelique does.'

'I wouldn't know,' he replied. 'Because I've never had sex with Anjelique.'

She tramped down on the idiotic surge of adrenaline. And decided she was definitely finished with her alcohol intake for the night.

But jolted, when he covered her hand, brushed his thumb across the knuckles. 'You, on the other hand...'

Her eyes met his and she felt a little dizzy—mesmerised by the cool blue of his irises.

'You wanna know the one thing I remember real clear from that night?' he murmured.

She shook her head, knowing she didn't want to know, especially not in that low seductive growl that was setting sparks off all over her sex-starved body.

'However wrong we were for doing it, it felt right while it lasted.'

Her pulse rate accelerated at the forceful tone. 'I don't think we should talk about that,' she whispered, her voice faltering along with her resistance. 'It's a really bad idea.'

He climbed off his stool, and pressed his hand to her

back—making the tingles hit meltdown as he rubbed the slinky silk over sensitised skin. He hooked her hair behind her ear and leaned in to whisper against her lobe. 'Bad ideas can lead to awesome sex.'

She shuddered, not caring any more that she was sitting in a public bar, or that she wanted to stretch against his palms like a contented cat.

'And it's not wrong any more,' he murmured, his breath hot and seductive against her ear.

She raised her head. 'Are you sure about that?' she said a little breathlessly, as it occurred to her just how far removed the Carter who stood before her now was from the innocent man she'd once seduced, if that cocksure look was anything to go by.

'I'm not dating right now—are you?' he said, deliberately misinterpreting the question.

'No, but.'

He pressed a thumb to her lips, silencing the feeble protest.

'Didn't you ever wonder what it would be like between us…without all the emotional garbage tripping us up?'

Emotional garbage.

She heard the words, and saw the harsh cynicism behind the hunger.

'Yes, I have,' she answered honestly, because there wasn't much point being coy when her desire had outstripped her caution a good half an hour ago.

Was she seriously considering this? And why couldn't she seem to consider anything else, such as running off screaming into the night, which had to be the smarter, safer, more sensible option?

He placed both his hands on her waist, and drew her off the stool, until she stood in his embrace, that spicy, musky scent intoxicating her. 'I have a whole hotel suite upstairs, if you want to find out the answer.'

'That would be insane,' she whispered. 'You're insane.' Why did he have to look so gorgeous and why couldn't she muster even a single iota of the guilt she should be feeling?

'And this would be relevant because…?' The quick feral grin sealed her fate.

Because suddenly she knew why she'd never been able to stop running from what had happened that night. It wasn't because of the mistakes they'd made, the bad things they'd done. She'd been punished a thousand times over for those and she'd changed enough to know she would never be that reckless, thoughtless girl again.

But she hadn't forgotten the glorious way he had made her feel either. He was the one that had got away. And she'd never been able to forget him. Not entirely.

And now he was back. And available. And this time, whatever they did together would just be about the sex. She could have him, enjoy him, get over the physical hunger that had burned inside her for years, and then let him and all the memories go, and walk away for good with no more nagging regrets.

Because if there was one thing she had learned in the years since that night—it was how to separate her sexual needs from her emotional ones.

'I guess it isn't relevant,' she murmured. 'Not any more.'

There was no Missy, no marriage in a fortnight, nothing to feel guilty about any more. And they both appeared to be two very different people now.

For whatever reason, Carter, the sensitive, conflicted, sex-deprived virgin had been replaced by Carter the cynical, commanding and sexually confident player. And, thanks to the devastation she'd had to face and overcome after their one night together—not to mention several thousand dollars' worth of therapy in the years since—she was no longer the screwed-up little flirt who thought having sex with any man who took her fancy could replace the love her father had denied her.

His thumbs pressed into the hollow of her hips as he brought his mouth close to hers. 'It was good then, but it'll be better now—because this time, we'll both know what the hell we're doing.'

She smiled, disarmed by the self-deprecating comment—even though she was sure it was disingenuous. 'Be careful, Carter,' she teased, the urge to flirt overwhelming her caution. 'You don't want to oversell yourself, because as I recall you were a remarkably precocious virgin....'

His answering chuckle arrowed through her. 'There's no doubting you were a powerful inspiration to me back then. But I've learned a few things since—about stamina and focus and technique.' He gave her bottom lip a playful nip, sending a delicious shiver down to her core. 'Which makes me confident I can do a lot better now.'

She let out a shaky breath, her arousal already long past the point of no return. 'Then I suppose the least I can do is let you prove it.'

'Amen to that.' He groaned, then clasped her cheeks in rough palms.

His mouth covered hers, his lips as hot and hungry as she remembered them. But this time he took control of the kiss. There was no tender, tentative, achingly sweet exploration, no moans of staggered arousal, just hot, insistent strokes as his tongue took possession of her mouth, and demanded her response.

She could vaguely hear the sounds of the bar around them—but the exhibitionist in her, that had never really gone away, had no problem wrapping her arms around Carter's waist, and letting her tongue duel with his, refusing to relinquish control and making her own demands in return.

Lust flowed on a heady wave down to her centre as he tried to force her surrender and she refused to submit.

'Hey, guys, you wanna get a room? We've got a whole hotel at your disposal here.'

They broke apart at the pained words from the bartender.

'Sure,' Carter replied as he threw several bills on the bar. 'You ready?' he asked as he grasped her hand.

She nodded. *As ready as I'll ever be.*

'Have a good evening, folks,' the bartender called after them, stuffing what Gina suspected was a hefty tip into his pocket.

She blew the guy a cheeky kiss, letting impulse take over as Carter led her out of the bar.

What harm could one night do, now? Carter Price was here and available—and hotter than ever. And they'd both changed so much from who they were then. But one thing had never changed. How easily he could send her senses reeling—until desire flowed through her veins like a heady drug. And if the only thing standing between her and complete closure was that lingering hunger—didn't she owe it to herself to give in to temptation one last time? And get a definitive answer to that question? Now she had the chance?

She'd waited ten years, for goodness' sake. Surely that was long enough?

She might have turned over a new leaf, but she wasn't a nun!

CHAPTER FIVE

Are you out of your freaking mind?

Carter clasped Gina's hand, headed across the lobby towards the elevators and felt as if he were charging back in time.

Ten years. Ten long, life-altering years since that one dumb act of self-destruction. And he hadn't learned a damn thing, because all he could think about, all he could focus on, was the urge to get into Gina Carrington's panties all over again.

The hunger that had gripped him as soon as he'd seen her sweeping through the hotel lobby—convinced she had to be some kind of weird erotic apparition brought on by jet lag and frustration—had been gnawing at his gut all night. He'd managed to dial down the intensity for two solid hours, talking about his business to keep his mind out of his pants—but the insistent ache had snapped and snarled throughout like an angry dog.

Every time she swung her head and that up-do threatened to tumble down. Every time she puckered up round her straw and he felt the tug in his groin. Every time her voice lowered to make a point and the sultry purr prickled over his skin like a cat testing its claws.

As the night had drawn on he'd gotten fixated on the ache, and accepted the fact there was no way in hell he was going to be able to walk away tonight.

The elevator took an eternity to creep up to the fifteenth floor crowded with tourists and businessmen and the woman standing beside him, whose fingers remained cool and firm in his. His grip tightened as they finally escaped the crush and he strode down the corridor towards his suite.

He heard a muffled curse behind him. 'Carter, slow down, before I break an ankle.'

He stopped as she stumbled on those killer heels. The urge to pick her up and throw her over his shoulder was so strong— he went with it. No way was he risking a broken ankle putting this booty call in jeopardy.

'Carter, what are you doing?' she yelped as he dipped, scooped her up and swung round, her legs flailing as her lush butt pressed into the side of his head. 'Put me down, for goodness' sake.'

'Not a chance.'

'I can walk!' The protest came out in breathless pants as her stomach rode his shoulder blade.

'Not fast enough for my liking.'

'This is so undignified,' she announced, but the husky laugh spurred him on, reminding him of the bad girl she'd been. Good to know that girl was still there beneath all the poise and professionalism—and the dumb apology.

He balanced her on his shoulder as he slipped his keycard into the slot on the door of his suite—amazed his fingers were steady enough to get the thing to work the first time.

Kicking the door open, he marched into the room and dropped her on her feet. The night-time view of the Hudson River displayed by the suite's glass walls had taken his breath away the first time he'd stayed at The Standard. It barely even registered now as all his attention zeroed in on the woman framed by the panoramic cityscape. An errant curl cupped one flushed cheek while her uneven breathing tightened the silk across that amazing rack. Right now, he could have been staying in a Motel 6 and he would have felt like a king.

He grabbed her wrist, dragged her to him. 'Come here.'

'I am here,' she announced, the haughty tone calling to his inner caveman.

He plucked the pins out of her hair, let the mass of soft brown hair cascade into his hands. 'I want it down.'

She laughed, shaking her head until the riot of curls bounced over her shoulders. 'Do you now,' she murmured, draping her arms round his neck and twisting a finger in the hair at his nape.

'Yeah.' He held her head, nipped at her bottom lip, then feasted on that soft mouth, his tongue thrusting deep—his hunger intensifying when she thrust back.

He pulled away, his breathing harsh at the sight of her reddened lips, the dark dilated pupils.

'When did you become such a Neanderthal?' she asked, her tongue licking the spot where he'd nipped her.

'When I had to talk business for two hours to stop myself jumping you on a barstool.'

'How intriguing. I had no idea you were thinking about sex while discussing how to grow business opportunities in a hostile investment environment.' She purred the words like a phone-sex operator. 'You sounded very informative.'

'It's called multitasking.' He reached up to find the zip on her dress, yanked it down with a sibilant hum. 'The whole time I was imagining you naked.'

She gave a husky laugh as the bodice drooped to reveal the scarlet lace of her bra.

'Well, maybe it's time you stopped imagining.'

She stood back to wiggle out of the silky shift. It pooled around her feet as his gaze devoured the sight of firm, full breasts, the delicious curve of waist and hip and those mile-long legs, her nakedness barely covered by the skimpy swatches of lace.

Lust seared through his system as the last of the blood left his brain.

'Hell, you're like a Victoria's Secret catalogue come to life.'

'A man who reads lingerie catalogues.' She laughed. 'You may be my perfect date.'

He dragged her close, let his palms skim over lush flesh and struggled not to hold her too tightly. He wanted to be inside her, right this second. But more than that, he wanted to make this good, better even than their first time. He wanted to savour her, to seduce her, to make her beg, the way she'd once made him beg.

'I hate to ruin my perfect-date status. But not a lot of reading went on. That catalogue's the equivalent of *Playboy* when you're a twelve-year-old boy,' he whispered against her neck and felt the shudder of response. 'But Victoria and her secrets are dead to me now I have the real thing in my hands.' He unhooked the lacy bra, threw it away, and cupped the heaving flesh in rough palms. She let out a slow moan as he rolled her nipples between his fingers and watched them stiffen.

He fastened his mouth on one engorged tip, made it swell and elongate beneath his tongue, revelling in the choked whimpers of her surrender.

Her fingers fisted in his hair and she jerked his head back. 'I want you naked too, Carter.'

He grinned at the eagerness, all traces of subtlety, of subterfuge, of teasing gone. But he didn't plan to make it that easy—not for him, and certainly not for her—despite the fact that the pounding in his pants was now painful. 'Not yet,' he said. 'Take the panties off.'

A tiny crease crossed her brow and her chin firmed. 'I don't take orders,' she announced, the act of defiance somewhat undermined by the heaving breasts and the erect nipples, glistening from his attention.

'Take them off, or I rip them off.' He let his gaze drift to the delicate red lace. 'Your call, but they look pricey.'

Her eyes narrowed, but then she laughed. 'You want them off, *you* take them off. Knickers aren't that easy to rip…' she began.

He twisted the delicate lace in his fist and tore. 'You were saying?' he murmured as he flung away the tattered remains of her pricey underwear.

Her eyes went round, but he caught the flash of shocked arousal lurking in the deep green depths.

That's right, sugar. I'm the one on top now.

'Those were worth fifty dollars,' she gasped in a breathy whisper that sounded more surprised than outraged.

'Not any more, they're not.' He curled a hand round her waist, yanked her back.

Her palms flattened on the front of his shirt, and he saw the spark of excitement, a split second before she gripped his collar—and ripped.

'Two can play at that game, big boy,' she purred as the sound of tearing cotton, buttons popping, filled the air.

But when she let go of the torn fabric to touch his bare skin, he grasped both her wrists, swung her round, banded his arms around her midriff, and held her captive. 'But only one of us can win.'

'What the…?' She struggled as he brought her flush against him and her naked buttocks nestled against the stiff ridge in his pants.

'No touching,' he commanded, nipping her ear lobe. 'Until I say so, sugar. I'm in charge this time.'

And he didn't intend to relinquish control. Until they'd both been burned to a crisp.

* * *

What the heck?

Gina squirmed against the immobilising forearm, but her movements only increased the friction, making her more aware of his big body surrounding her—and what felt like a two-by-four nestled against her bottom. She stilled, sure she could feel the massive erection barely contained by his trousers swelling even more. And wondered how the hell she'd got into this position.

Trapped, vulnerable, overpowered and impossibly aroused.

'Look at yourself.' The low command whispered against her ear, the shiver of awareness skittering down her spine. Heat flushed through her as she lifted her head and saw the shocking reflection in the glass wall that looked out across the dark expanse of the Hudson River.

Moonlight illuminated her naked body—which glowed an unearthly white but for the stiff rosy nipples and the neatly trimmed raven curls at the apex of her thighs. Her pale shape contrasted sharply with the tall dark figure holding her captive—still fully clothed but for the glimpse of chest she'd exposed.

She gasped, shocked not just by the wanton view, but the fierce surge of desire. 'For goodness' sake, Carter, draw the blinds or something.' She fought his embrace. 'The whole of Manhattan can see us.'

She might be an exhibitionist, but she didn't want to get arrested.

'Settle down.' He chuckled, the sound thick with arrogance and amusement. 'The glass is treated. No one can see you but me.'

She stopped wriggling, far too aware of his forearm flexing under her breasts, the chest hairs prickling against her back and the rod of steel that pressed into her buttocks.

'And I intend to enjoy every single inch,' he murmured as

he lifted her limp arm and placed it around his neck, making her breasts thrust forward.

She swallowed, her throat parched as her eyes watched herself in the glass—mesmerised by the sensual image, and the harsh demand in his gaze as his eyes met hers. Suddenly this wasn't a game any more.

Shock and excitement burned away on a surge of lust so fierce, so all-consuming, she felt woozy.

He drew his thumb down the inside of her arm, making her whole body quiver as sensation arrowed to her centre. His forearm tightened around her waist, holding her upright for the delicate torment, as seeking fingers circled her breast, exploring in maddeningly slow circles.

She moaned, stretching into the teasing caress. 'You need to hurry up,' she demanded. 'Before I explode.'

He plucked at her nipple. The pinch was painless, but hard enough to send darts of sensation spiralling to her yearning sex. And make her cry out.

'Patience, grasshopper,' he whispered. 'Or you will be punished.'

A hoarse laugh popped out of her mouth—her mind dazed by the slow torture, and the unbearably erotic threat.

'Shh.' His lips nuzzled the soft skin of her neck. 'We've hardly even started.'

'Oh, God!' She jolted against the restraining forearm as his torturous touch left her breasts and trailed down. His fingertips caressed, stroked, seduced, but so slowly, she knew she'd probably die of anticipation before they got where she needed them to be.

'Please…' she sobbed as her belly shivered, each tormenting caress sending a new pulse of heat to her core.

'Please what, sugar?' he mocked, the thick molasses of his accent scraping at the last of her resistance. 'Please stop?'

'Don't you dare!' she demanded, her voice hoarse with

desperation as his fingers teased the curls that hid her sex, but stopped short of their goal.

Her eyelids fluttered open. She stared at their reflection, registering the dark hand so close to heaven and yet so far—and the feral arousal on his face.

Who was this guy?

'Tell me what you want,' he said, his voice strained but firm, 'and you just might get it. If you ask me real nice.'

'Touch me.'

'That's not nearly nice enough,' he mocked, still teasing her with his circling fingers.

'Touch me, please.'

She writhed as his fingers delved into the slick folds. At last. He swept across her swollen clitoris and the coil of desire tightened unbearably.

'That's not...' She protested, frustration rising and intensifying the need as he retreated again. Why wasn't he touching her *there*?

'That's not what?' She heard it then, the smug hint of amusement. 'Maybe you need to beg?' he teased.

'Oh for...' She bit off a curse, held back from that glorious oblivion by an invisible thread—that only he could cut. 'Will you just touch my...'

She cried out, the tirade interrupted as blunt fingers stroked over the burning nub.

'Touch you there, huh?'

She writhed, bucked, giving him his answer as he caressed the perfect spot—and she hurtled towards oblivion under the exquisite torture.

'Come for me, Gina.'

The wave crested, and broke in a shattering shower of bright white sensation, as if brought forth by his command. Then flowed over her in one glorious surge after the other as he stroked at the heart of her—in the perfect place, at the perfect pace—beckoning her up and over again.

His hand withdrew and she sagged against him, hollowed out, exhausted, by the staggering intensity of her orgasm, and the fight to maintain some control over her own body—and his effect on it.

A fight she was pretty sure she'd just lost. Completely.

Rousing herself, she swung round as his forearm loosened. And grabbed hold of his shirt, tearing the remains of it off his shoulders, determined to regain some of the lost ground.

She threw the tattered cotton over her shoulder. 'Oh, dear, look what I did to your shirt,' she mocked. 'I guess I won't charge you for the panties.'

'Damn straight you won't,' he replied, not looking cowed in the least. 'That shirt cost me over two hundred dollars. So I figure you owe me.'

She allowed herself a moment to absorb the breath-taking display of tanned skin and bulging muscles—before making quick work of his belt buckle. And drawing down the zip to reveal the huge bulge straining against his boxers. Her eyes met his and she cupped the firm package. 'Then it must be payback time.'

So what if he could seduce her into a coma? Didn't mean she couldn't seduce him right back.

'Yeah, I guess it is,' he said, the challenge in his cobalt eyes unmistakeable. 'Give it your best shot, sugar.' The low chuckle was as smug as ever as he kicked off the rest of his clothes, and stood before her gloriously naked.

She took a few extra moments to get her breath back.

Goodness.

His body had matured, the once lean, coltish physique gaining muscle bulk in all the right places—making his shoulders broader, the V of his hipbones more defined, his triceps and biceps a lot more prominent and the ridged six-pack quite simply awe-inspiring.

Someone had been working out. A lot.

She touched a nail to the new swirls of chest hair that now surrounded his flat brown nipples and then traced the happy trail down to the thicket where his erection jutted out.

Oh, my word.

Was it her imagination, or had that got even more magnificent too?

'Carter, you're beautiful,' she said, running her tongue over her lips as she dropped to her knees. She smiled up at him, adrenaline surging through her veins like a heady drug as she circled his girth, felt it twitch against her palm—and saw the fierce flash of need cross his face. 'Brace yourself, sugar,' she purred, mimicking his lazy, moonlit and magnolia tones. And then swept her tongue from the root to the tip and heard him moan.

Holy hell!

Carter ran his fingers into her hair, caressing her scalp, as his knees turned to Jell-O and the fire in his gut became an inferno.

Stay upright, damn it.

He dragged his gaze away from the sight of those soft, full lips surrounding him, and struggled to take the exquisite punishment like a man. But then he saw their reflection—and the decadent image of Gina on her knees, pleasuring him with her mouth, nearly had him collapsing in a heap.

She should have looked submissive as she knelt before him, but instead she looked bold and defiant, like an Amazon goddess, feeding into every schoolboy sex fantasy he'd ever had about her. And he'd had a heck of a lot of those over the years.

Hellfire and damnation.

That was where he was headed and he didn't care.

He tried to force his mind to engage in banalities to stem the tidal wave of his orgasm and keep from disgracing himself. Against shuttered lids, he conjured a picture of the Sunday service at Riverbend Church; the board of directors of the Mill discussing the end of year's report...but every single image crashed and burned to be replaced by the glorious sight he'd glimpsed in the dark glass as her tongue licked and swirled, her mouth suckled. An image he feared would now be lasered into his brain for ever more.

He groaned, the heat curling and twisting and then yanking hard in his groin as her hot, beautiful mouth feasted on the last few ounces of his self-control.

His fingers tightened in the mass of curls as he dragged himself away from her. 'Enough.' Hooking his hands under her arms, he hoisted her off her knees.

Her cheeks pinkened as those bright green eyes flickered with challenge. 'Why did you stop me? I was enjoying myself.' The pouting lips made the heat pulse and throb harder.

He grabbed her wrist as she reached for him. 'Uh-uh. I said enough.'

She cocked one perfectly plucked eyebrow. 'Why? From all that moaning you were doing, I got the definite impression you were enjoying it too.'

He grinned. Damned if she wasn't as wild and reckless and wanton as she'd ever been beneath that layer of chic sophistication—and didn't that make her perfect for him? In the only way that mattered now.

'I didn't say I wasn't enjoying it,' he said, his gaze steady and his voice firm, or as firm as it could be while he was clinging onto control by his fingertips. 'I just don't want to come that way. Not this time.'

'Spoilsport.'

He laughed, but tightened his hold on her wrist and brought her fingers to his lips. 'I want to be inside you, Gina. I want to watch you climax with me—you're even more gorgeous when you come.'

He kissed her knuckles and a wary look crossed her face, giving him another disarming glimpse of the girl he remembered, who had been so bold sexually, and yet so unsure at the slightest sign of tenderness.

She draped her arms over his shoulders, threaded her fingers into his hair to drag him close, the siren returning full force—and he dismissed the sentimental thought. After all, there was nothing tender about tonight, and what he planned to do to her.

'Well, all you had to do was say so, Rhett,' she purred.

Brushing the riotous hair back from her face, he kissed her long and hard, thrusting his tongue into her mouth and forcing her to submit this time.

Cupping her generous butt in his hands, he boosted her into his arms, dumped her onto the room's kingsize bed. 'Consider yourself told.'

Gina laughed, the desire coursing through her veins and the electric connection that snapped to life between them making her feel free and unencumbered for the first time in a long time. It felt so good to relinquish control, to be able to take what she wanted without fearing the consequences.

Carter wouldn't judge her, because he knew who and what she really was. When it came to sex—hot, hard, explosive sex—they had always been kindred spirits.

He bracketed her hips and pressed his lips to her pulse point, drawing her knees up and positioning himself above her—but as she took in a deep lungful of that tangy masculine scent the press of his erection registered. The intoxicating desire ripped away to be replaced by a jolt of panic. Slapping her hands against his shoulders, she forced him back.

'Wait, Carter. You have to use protection.'

He lifted his head, his eyes a little unfocused, a little dazed.

'Please tell me you have something with you, because I don't,' she continued, the panic making her voice hitch. She should have said something sooner, much sooner. Why hadn't she?

'Yeah, sure. Sorry.' He raked a hand through his hair. 'Wait right there.' He jumped off the bed and padded to the suite's bathroom, his naked butt gilded by the moonlight.

She stared at the ceiling, the sudden realisation of what they'd almost done—a second time—dousing the flames.

He reappeared in the doorway of the bathroom. Her pulse hammered at the imposing sight silhouetted in the doorway. But as he returned to her she was hurled back to a time in her life that had left her hollow and empty and devastated. A time she had forced herself never to acknowledge. She sat up, threw her legs over the bed.

'I have to go,' she said, struggling to keep her voice steady as the brutal memory hovered too close, threatening to engulf her.

'Why?' He caught her wrist, preventing her from moving as he sat beside her. 'I found what we needed.'

He threw a handful of foil packets on the bedside table.

'That's great. But we don't need them now. This was a mistake.'

She braced herself, ready for him to object, to call her names—it wouldn't be the first time she'd been branded a tease or worse. And given how his arousal didn't seem to have abated one bit he would probably have a point. But right now she was too busy protecting herself to worry about any injuries she might have caused him.

But to her surprise, instead of getting angry or annoyed, he lifted a palm and cupped her cheek. 'Why is it a mistake all of a sudden?'

She shook her head to dislodge the possessive touch—this

was fine when it was just sex, but she didn't want to risk getting her emotions involved. 'No reason.'

She tried to rise again, but he simply held her waist, making it impossible for her to move without getting into a wrestling match—something she definitely didn't intend to do, because, while her head was telling her clearly making love with Carter Price would be a very bad idea now, she couldn't rely on her body to play ball.

'There is a reason,' he replied in that CEO tone he'd been using all evening. She'd found it a major turn on during foreplay; she was finding it somewhat less so now. 'And you need to tell me what it is.'

'No, actually, I don't. I'm under no obligation to—'

'Think again, Gina,' he interrupted. 'Because you're not going anywhere until you do.'

She sucked in a breath, trying to remain patient and sensible, and stave off a hissy fit.

'I'm sorry,' she said, her voice tight with the effort to sound conciliatory. 'I realise you're still extremely aroused…' She flicked her gaze to his crotch and heat crept up her neck at the sight of the magnificent erection. 'And that's obviously partly my fault…'

'*Partly?*' he interrupted, giving an incredulous laugh.

She looked away as the heat hit her cheeks. For Pete's sake, was she actually blushing? She never blushed.

'Okay, fine, *mostly* my fault,' she added, in the interests of complete disclosure. Because she'd never been coy either. 'But that doesn't mean I have to sleep with you if I don't want to.'

He cursed. 'Give me some credit here. I'm not a kid, any more. I do have some control. And I would never expect any woman to sleep with me if she didn't want to—no matter how aroused she's gotten me. I may not be the gentleman my mama raised me to be, but I'm not that much of jerk.'

'Okay, good,' she said, relief flowing through her. He

sounded more affronted than angry. Not that she cared if
he was angry, she told herself staunchly; she'd never had a
problem dealing with male tantrums. But right now she felt
too exposed to relish dealing with one from him. 'Then I'd
like to leave.'

She waited, but, instead of releasing her, he began to stroke
his thumbs back and forth over the skin beneath her ribs, in
a light caress that sent darts of sensation places she really
didn't want them.

'Carter, let go of my waist,' she said, breathlessly.

'Not until I get an explanation. What made you change
your mind?'

She couldn't tell him that. Would never tell him that. Because it would mean revealing something she had decided a
long time ago he had never really been a part of. The pregnancy had been an accident, a biological blip, that had ended
almost as soon as it had begun—and forced her to re-evaluate
who she was and what she was. But she'd come out the other
side. She hadn't thought about it in years. And if she could
get away from him, she wouldn't have to think about it now.

She sent him what she hoped was a bored look. 'It doesn't
seem spontaneous any more. And I'm really not that turned
on now.'

'You're really not, huh?' His mouth curled on one side and
she saw the sceptical gleam in his eye. 'Why are you lying?'

'I'm not.'

She'd always been an exceptionally convincing liar—after
all, she'd had a lot of practice in her teens—but unfortunately
as she said the words her lungs seized as if all the oxygen had
been sucked out of them at once—and the denial came out
on an unconvincing hum.

'How about we test that theory?' His voice deepened as his
hands stroked down her naked thighs and gripped her knees.

'If you were any kind of a gentleman, you'd take my word

for it,' she murmured, pushing the words out past the constriction in her throat as he parted her legs. A move she appeared powerless to resist as her centre throbbed in anticipation.

'That's true enough.' His thumbs blazed a trail of goosebumps, caressing the sensitive skin of her inner thigh as his hands headed back towards heaven. 'And if you were any kind of a lady, you wouldn't lie about it.'

'I'm not lying.' Those damn thumbs angled across the juncture of her legs, and caressed—back and forth, back and forth—making the protest compete with the telltale hitch in her breathing.

Kneeling in front of her, he pushed her thighs wider and let his thumbs touch the slick swollen folds. She braced her hands on the bed, let her head fall back and struggled to breathe as all thought, all feeling, all memory burned away in a blaze of lust.

'There now. You seem to like that well enough, sugar.'

She could hear the arrogance and the amusement and she would have objected, but all she cared about now was concentrating on the heat, and forgetting the rest. The orgasm fluttered towards her on soaring wings as he used his thumbs to hold her open and then licked at the heart of her.

She sobbed, the sound echoing back at her off the room's hard, designer surfaces. Then he fastened his lips on her swollen clitoris and sucked. She screamed. Soaring straight into the cosmos.

The orgasm slammed into her, radiating out through her belly, her breasts, her fingers and toes. She collapsed back on the bed as he stood above her. He grabbed the foil packet, ripped it with his teeth, rolled on the condom, then sat on the bed and hauled her up, to straddle his lap.

She held onto his shoulders as his hands cupped her buttocks and positioned her over the huge erection.

'I want to be inside you, Gina.' The naked need in his eyes

matched the strain in his voice, the tendons standing out on his neck, and sweat slicking his brow. But still he held her poised above him, and made no move to take her. 'Don't make us wait any longer.'

She impaled herself in one smooth stroke—the staggering fullness making her head snap back, her fingers clutch at his shoulders. And then she began to move. Rising up, sinking back, the intimate stroking touching that place deep inside that only he had ever reached.

'That feels so damn good,' he coaxed, urging her on, guiding her movements, the wild ride racing them both towards oblivion.

She cried out, her nails digging into muscle, her breathing ragged, the exquisite pleasure becoming too close to pain as she hurtled over—with him this time.

Gina let the blissful fatigue of afterglow wash over her as she collapsed on top of his big body.

Carter Price hadn't been boasting. He'd certainly perfected his technique since their first merry meeting, not to mention his stamina.

'Damn, woman. That was something else,' he murmured as he swept the curtain of her hair away from his face, and kissed her.

'Hmm,' she hummed in agreement, rolling off him.

She let out a weary laugh at his heartfelt moan as she crawled up the bed, her arms and legs more than a little shaky.

'Hey, come back here,' he declared, as he hauled himself up. 'Where are you going?'

'Nowhere at the moment,' she replied as she flopped back onto the pillows, her whole body pleasantly numb. 'You've rendered me senseless.'

'Then we're even.'

She lay back on the stack of plump pillows, gazed out of

the glass wall, and tracked the tiny lights of the tourist boats plying their trade across the bay. How foolish to think that this had ever been about anything other than sex.

Carter joined her, dragging the quilt folded over the foot of the bed up to cover them, then wrapped an arm around her shoulders to draw her to his side.

She would have objected to the possessive gesture. She generally didn't snuggle after sex. But she let it pass for now, because she wasn't entirely sure she was capable of coordinated movement. And he smelt delicious.

She rested her head on his shoulder as his arm tightened. And took in a lungful of that unique scent. Soap and pheromones and man, now layered with the tangy aroma of sex. She squeezed her thighs together, a little disturbed by the renewed pulse of arousal.

No way. She couldn't have another orgasm tonight. Or she'd pass out. Plus she needed to consider leaving soon.

His fingers delved into her hair, lifting and separating the strands and making her scalp tingle. 'So now we've got proof,' he murmured, the words low and intimate in the dark room

'Proof of what?' she asked, around a huge yawn.

'Proof our first time was no fluke.'

She stiffened, not liking where this might be leading. Or the confidential tone of his voice. 'It wasn't my first time, remember,' she said. 'It was yours.'

His hand stilled on the back of her head. 'Why are you so hung up about that?'

She tapped her fingers on his chest. 'Hung up about what?'

'You know what. That you were my first.'

'That's ridiculous, of course I'm not,' she said, but could hear that telltale hitch in her breathing. Damn, why couldn't she lie around Carter with any conviction? It was as if he had injected her with truth serum.

He remained silent for a while, making her wonder if

maybe she'd got away with it, but then he said, 'It wasn't that big a deal back then, and it sure isn't any kind of deal now.'

She levered herself up, stared down into his handsome face. 'Then why were you getting all sentimental about "our first time" a minute ago?' She did air quotes.

His lips quirked, the sensual smile making her heart flip over in her chest. Damn it, why did he have to be so ludicrously sexy?

'You mistake me, Gina.' He bunched her hair at the back of her neck and gave it a tug, forcing her head back and making her breasts more accessible. He covered one with his palm. 'That wasn't sentiment.' His gaze drifted to her breast as he toyed with the nipple. 'That was purely an observation about our sexual compatibility.'

'I see...' The tension coiled in her abdomen as he rose up on his elbow, forcing her back into the pillows. She gasped as he captured the beaded nipple with his lips and drew it into his mouth. The hot flow of lust and endorphins charged into her sex, making her arch off the bed and the still tender spot between her thighs throb painfully. 'Carter, stop,' she hissed, her hands fisting on the bed sheets. 'I really can't do it again so soon...'

And how on earth could he?

'Sure you can,' he countered, before getting back to the business of proving her wrong.

CHAPTER SIX

GINA WINCED AT the blast of light on her retinas, before awareness of the big body wrapped around hers yanked her the rest of the way out of dreamland. Slow, steady breathing stirred the hair on the back of her head, a heavy forearm lay across her midriff, and something indisputably long and solid nestled against her backside.

Good grief, I'm spooning with Carter Price—and he's hard as a rock. Again!

The memory of the torrid hours they'd spent before dawn came tumbling back. The man had the stamina and fortitude of a prize stallion—and he'd learned a great deal, in the years since she'd popped his cherry. She dismissed the foolish punch of her pulse at the realisation that while she might have been Carter's first, she certainly hadn't been his last.

No wonder she felt limp and sated—she edged across the mattress, testing the tender spot between her thighs—and frankly rather sore.

The heavy forearm tightened as a large hand cupped her breast and gave it a friendly squeeze. 'Morning, sugar.'

The husky murmur, heavy with sleep, had her shifting round to glance over her shoulder.

'You're awake?' With his eyes closed, his wavy hair delightfully rumpled, what looked like a two-day shadow on his jaw and his mobile mouth sporting the hint of a smile, it was hard to tell.

One eyelid lifted, the cobalt-blue gleaming in the light from the bay. His lips twisted into the full megawatt smile. 'Can't you tell?' His erection nudged her bottom.

She laughed, a little nervously. 'Forget it, Rhett. After the night we had, I'm not going to be operational for at least a week.'

The warm palm strayed from her breast to curl over her hip and stroke. 'You sure about that?'

She wasn't, not in the slightest, if the heat surging through her was anything to go by, but she didn't plan to negotiate. Because where Carter was concerned, her will power came a very poor second to her libido. And unfortunately he knew it, from the wicked grin as the stroking hand migrated to her backside.

Swiping his hand away, she flung the quilt back and bolted off the bed. 'I have to get going.' She checked the clock on his bedside table. 'I'm meeting the Awesomes at a bridal boutique in Brooklyn at eleven for a bridesmaid's fitting and I can't be late.'

'Now who's the spoilsport?' He propped himself on the pillows.

She scooped her now hopelessly wrinkled dress off the floor and held it over her nakedness, a little too aware of his patient watchful gaze as she hunted up the rest of her clothing.

'Do you mind if I use your shower?' she asked, ignoring the sizzle in her breasts as he tucked a folded arm behind his head, apparently settling in to enjoy the show.

'Sure. You want company?'

'Better not,' she said quickly as the sizzle went into overdrive and she grabbed her bra from its resting place hooked onto the corner of the room's huge plasma TV. 'I can't imagine sharing a shower with you will be particularly time efficient.' She spotted the remains of her Indian lace knickers and picked them off the satellite console. Heat flushed through her at the memory of Carter ripping them off her the night before.

'Damn it.'

How on earth was she going to explain a complete absence of underwear to her pals in the changing room? It was already nine-fifty. She didn't have time to get all the way back to her apartment in Red Hook. Maybe she could stop off at a department store on the way to the Manhattan Bridge Overpass District, where Amber's boutique was situated? Or have a quiet word with Reese's friend when she arrived? Did bridal boutiques sell emergency underwear?

'Will my sister be there?'

She stared at Carter, momentarily confused by the question until he added, 'Could you get her to give me a call? We need to set up a meet while I'm in town.'

And then the stupidity of what she'd done hit her right between the eyes—like a cold hard slap, knocking the breath out of her lungs and making the back of her neck feel as if someone had yanked out all the small hairs.

The remains of her knickers dropped from her numbed fingers.

After six months of celibacy—and confining herself to the automative delights of Justin, her trusty vibrator—she'd come tumbling off the wagon with the one man guaranteed to screw up the friendship she'd spent most of the summer trying to repair.

Not that she hadn't considered this last night. Fleetingly, and through a haze of hormones.... But now, suddenly, it didn't feel nearly so defensible. Of course it wasn't any of Marnie's business who her brother slept with, especially now that Carter was a free man and no longer bound in matrimony to Marnie's best friend—and she very much doubted that even if Marnie knew about what they'd spent the night doing together she would make a fuss. She was far too mature and pragmatic and, well, polite for that.

But sleeping with Marnie's big brother again suddenly felt hopelessly tacky and immature.

It wasn't exactly a great way to restore Marnie's trust in her as a person and as a friend.... Nor would it do much for Marnie's already rocky relationship with her brother. Which Gina knew had been set on its current course as a result of their first indiscretion ten years ago.

'What's the matter? Is it the panties?' Carter asked, then reached for the hotel phone. 'Don't sweat it. I'll order you a new pair.'

'No, don't, it's not that, it's...' She blinked at the tattered lace now resting on her big toe. Her stomach began to feel tight and achy, the way it always had in the past when she'd gone too far. She put her hand up, to stop him dialling the concierge. 'Marnie *will* be there, at the boutique.'

'Yeah, I know.' He didn't look remotely surprised or concerned as he placed the handset back in its cradle. 'You said the Awesomes. That's what you guys used to call yourselves, right? You and Marnie and Reese and the mousy geek girl.'

'Cassie's not a geek, she's just brilliant, and, considering she's about to marry Sam "Tuck" Tucker, the football player, I'd say mousy is the new hot.'

And they'd called themselves the Awesome Foursome, because their friendship had been Awesome. Awesome for her at least. Until that year in college, she'd never had any close female friendships—her mother had died when she was so young she didn't remember her and she'd always seen the other girls at school as competition. But during her year at Hillbrook she'd come to realise how important female friendships could be. And then she'd gone and torpedoed it.

But she wanted it to be Awesome again. Truly awesome.

And that meant regaining Marnie's trust. But how could she do that, if Marnie found out about her and Carter?

'The NFL quarterback?' Carter gave a low whistle, sounding impressed. 'Still waters, huh?'

'Yes, precisely,' she muttered, gathering her clothes to her breasts again, when Carter's gaze dipped noticeably.

'Damn, are you sure you've got to run off? How about I text Marnie, tell her you're going to be late?'

'No!' she yelped, she actually yelped—as all the blood headed out of her brain and exploded into her heart. 'You can't do that.'

The crease on his brow became a furrow. 'Why not? I've gotta arrange to meet her some time this week anyhow.' The sexy smile returned as he reached for the hem of her dress, gave it a playful tug. 'And it'd give me time to order you up some new panties. And help you wash your hair.'

She yanked the dress out of his fingers. Was he completely insane? 'You're not telling Marnie about this. About us. About last night,' she clarified when he continued to look at her as if she'd just sprouted an extra head. 'You can't.'

'Why can't I?'

'Because I don't want her to know, obviously.'

'Obviously. my butt. Why don't you want her to know? It's not like she doesn't know I have sex,' he added, apropos to absolutely nothing.

'Yes, but she doesn't know you've just had sex with me, does she?'

'Not yet, she doesn't.' He grasped her hand, dragged her back towards the bed. 'But I don't plan to keep it a secret. Why would I?'

She tugged her hand free, cursing the heat shimmying up her spine. 'Because Marnie doesn't need to know.'

'That doesn't answer my question,' he said, an annoyingly astute look crossing his face.

'Please, as a favour to me, Carter,' she said, trying her best puppy-dog pout. 'Don't tell Marnie about us. I said some pretty hideous things to her when this happened the first time. And I really don't want to revisit that situation in any shape or form.'

He shrugged. 'Okay, I guess it's no skin off my—'

'Pinkie swear,' she begged, keen to get a commitment out of him. But when she demonstrated the technique by crossing her own pinkie over her heart and kissing the tip, his brows lowered ominously.

'Don't push it, Carrington. I don't do pinkie swears.'

'Why not?'

'Because it's girlie and I'm a guy.' His lips lifted into a sly grin. 'You want me to prove it?'

'Absolutely not.' She stepped out of his reach, before he could kick off yet more sizzles and shimmies. 'I have to shower. Alone,' she added for good measure when he chuckled.

She needed to make a quick getaway now—no matter how much she might be tempted to stay. Sleeping with Carter again had been a mistake, on a lot of levels, however great it might have felt at the time. Not least of which was that he was a man she didn't seem to be able to wrap around her finger as easily as every other man she'd ever dated. Getting him to say he wouldn't mention this to Marnie was the best she could hope for. They wouldn't be doing this again. As he would be safely back in Savannah by the end of the week, and she would be steering well clear of him—and his addictive pheromones—until then.

'Aren't you forgetting something, sugar?'

She swung round at the laconic question. 'No, I don't think so.'

'My little sister's not as clueless about carnal relations as she used to be.' His gaze dipped pointedly to her bare bottom. 'I'm guessing she may well figure out something's up when you show up with no panties on.'

He laughed, obviously enjoying her distress immensely.

'Oh, go to hell…' she huffed, waltzing back towards the bathroom.

'Your butt looks real cute when you're mad.'

She shot him the finger and slammed the bathroom door to cut off the sound of his full-bodied laughter. But as she dropped the dress and stepped into the enormous power shower her whole body started to shake.

Last night's activities had the potential to be a disaster.… Not just because Marnie might find out—but because she was going to have to keep well away from Carter for the next seven days. And after the night they'd just shared, that was going to be a very tall order.

'What were you thinking?' she snapped at herself as the hot water hit her full in the face.

This didn't just have the potential to be a disaster, it already was one. And like every other disaster in her life so far, it was entirely of her own making.

Carter's laughter subsided as he picked up the hotel phone. 'Give me the concierge.'

Damn, but she fascinated him. She got worked up about the weirdest things. Marnie wouldn't care about them now. His sister was hardly the starry-eyed little romantic she'd once been, any more than he was the big brother she'd once looked up to. And while he'd always regretted her finding out he wasn't the man she thought he was the way she had—he didn't see why he, or Gina, should have to tiptoe around Marnie's sensibilities now.

His kid sister had been living in New York for five years—making her own way in the big bad Yankee city and steadfastly refusing to let him have any kind of foothold in her life. He was proud of Marnie and what she'd achieved—even though he'd never tell her, because she'd only accuse him of patronising her. But the point was, she'd moved on, made a life for herself away from Savannah, and she sure as hell didn't care about his love life any more. So why was Gina so hung up on Marnie finding out about them?

He shrugged off the thought as he got patched through to the concierge. Women. Who knew why they got hung up on half the stuff they got hung up on?

He made the request to the concierge and included a powerful incentive if it could be fulfilled in the next twenty minutes. He figured if Gina was like all the other women he'd ever dated, it would be a miracle if she was out of the bathroom before then.

Listening to the sound of running water, he imagined that lush body slick with soap suds. Heat pooled in his groin, and his morning erection perked right up.

He had to head off to The Waldorf for a lunch meeting with some Chinese investors, so it was probably a good thing he hadn't been able to persuade Gina to blow off her friends.

Resigned to the fact that he'd have to take a rain check for their next booty call at least until tonight, he hunted up a pair of sweat pants and a T-shirt from his suitcase. Dialling room service, he ordered breakfast and coffee and then stood by the glass wall to contemplate the awesome view—and the low-level hum of endorphins still cruising through his system.

He rubbed his palm across his midriff. He hadn't felt this sated and well rested and energised in years. Despite the fact that at a rough estimate he'd totalled about three hours' sleep in the last twenty-four.

And he gave Gina credit for that.

She really was his ideal sexual partner. He'd thought he'd been imagining how good they'd been together that night. But that night had only been a taster.

She was as wild and insatiable in the sack as he was, and even more wary of commitment out of it. He'd heard the caution in her voice when he'd asked any personal questions, felt her discomfort when he hugged her after sex, could tell she'd been reluctant to fall asleep in his arms, until he'd exhausted her—and himself. And he had a feeling this dumb notion about Marnie finding out was just another of her tactics for keeping a safe distance. She might even have persuaded herself her friendship with Marnie was a good excuse to call a halt to things.

Not gonna happen, sugar.

It was just plain dumb to throw a physical connection this perfect away over something so insubstantial.

The two of them were the perfect match. Last night had proved it beyond any reasonable and several unreasonable doubts. Having spent five torturous years suppressing his more basic sexual urges so his wife wouldn't freak out on him—and then five more trying to find someone who was happy to satisfy those needs without demanding more—he knew how rare Gina was.

He'd found her once and lost her, because of some dumb notion that he was a better man than his daddy. That he could be the marrying kind if he put his mind to it. Well, he'd been there, done that, and now had the decree absolute and a few thousand dollars a month in alimony payments to show for it.

He didn't plan to make the same mistake twice. He wasn't the marrying kind. But he did have a healthy sex drive—which he now had the chance to indulge in for a whole week with a woman who enjoyed sex as down and dirty as he did.

So he didn't plan to let Gina go so easily a second time. Not until they'd gotten their fill of each other while he was in New York. And whatever weird notions Gina had about Marnie—she could forget trying to persuade him they'd got their fill of each other in one night.

Something he would have to make clear to her, when she finally stopped hiding out in his shower.

Of course, he should probably ask her nicely instead of telling her. That would be the polite Southern thing to do. Especially as he knew how ornery she could be.

He saw the slow smile forming on his lips reflected in the glass.

Forget it.

He wasn't a gentleman. And he'd stopped asking nicely when he'd figured out that nice wasn't part of his nature.

And anyhow, taming Gina and that quick-fire temper of hers was all part of the attraction. She might have a history of wrapping men round her perfectly manicured pinkie— him included, once upon a time—but he was more than man enough to take her on today.

And harnessing all that fire and passion would make this wild ride even wilder.

Gina dashed into the bedroom of Carter's suite almost an hour later to find him flicking through *The Wall Street Journal* with the remains of his breakfast in front of him.

It had taken her longer than she'd planned to shower, wash and dry her hair, put on a semblance of decent make-up from the inadequate emergency supply in her purse and steam out the wrinkles in her dress—not to mention formulate exactly what she was going to say and how she was going to say it so that she could end her night of madness as quickly and cleanly and with as little fuss as possible. She had to pitch the brush-off just right. Most of all, she didn't want Carter getting any ideas that her refusal to see him again was in any way a challenge. Because if there was one thing she'd learned during their epic sex session last night, the new Carter, not unlike the old Carter, was a man with a sizeable ego and a well-honed competitive spirit—who was not a good loser.

Unfortunately, the fact that she'd spent an extra twenty minutes in the bathroom than she'd bargained for meant she was going to have to do all that in ten minutes flat—if she didn't want to turn up for her fitting more than half an hour late, and encourage even more probing questions from her friends.

'There you are.' He folded the paper on his plate. 'I ordered you up some breakfast, but it arrived a while back. It may be a mite cold now.'

He lifted the silver dome on the plate opposite to reveal a splendid assortment of freshly cut fruit, waffles and syrup. Saliva pooled under her tongue. 'I'm sorry, I really don't have time to do that justice. Maybe just a quick cup of coffee?'

'Sure thing.' He plopped the dome back over her breakfast, apparently unconcerned by her refusal, and picked up the silver pot next to his plate.

Maybe this was going to be easier than she had assumed. The heady aroma of fresh coffee filled the air as he poured her a cup. 'Cream and sugar, sugar?' he teased.

'Black's fine.' She took the cup, gulped the bitter liquid down, not quite as pleased with his nonchalant tone as she probably should be.

After fortifying herself. She popped the cup back on the table and toed on her stilettos. 'Well, I guess this is goodbye, then?' she said, feeling stupidly nervous all of a sudden. 'It was quite a night.'

'It sure was,' he said, his gaze roaming over her and making all the sizzles and shimmers buzz like alarm bells.

'Right, I'll just…' She shot a thumb over her shoulder. 'Leave.'

She headed for the door. She hadn't given him a single word of her carefully planned speech. Because she obviously hadn't needed to. Clearly she was just another of the many, many notches on his bedpost.

'Hold up, Gina.'

She swung round, the odd leap in her heart completely counterproductive, but there nonetheless. 'Yes?'

'I got you something.' He lifted a pale blue paper bag off the bed with the logo of an exclusive designer boutique on the front and handed it to her.

She took the package, somewhat dazed by the intensity of his gaze. Why had he bought her a gift? And why was her heart practically beating its way through her chest wall?

Opening the bag, she lifted out a pair of exquisite red lace panties—and laughed. 'Oh…' She didn't know what to say—at once touched that he would have thought of it, and turned on, as she suddenly became one hundred per cent more conscious of her current lack of underwear. 'Thank you. That was very thoughtful of you.'

'Not really.' His lips curved into a tempting grin. 'More like a necessity. That's a mighty short dress. I don't want anyone else getting a load of your naked butt but me.'

The blush fired up her neck. As heat swelled in her sex. Dropping the bag, she slipped her shoes off, and shimmied the red lace up her legs to cover her naked butt before she got any ideas about that teasing grin and the husky tone of his voice.

Not gonna happen, Gina. You're wearing your big girl panties now.

Grabbing her purse, she pressed her palm to his cheek, rubbed it over the rough stubble and gave him a quick kiss on the lips—keeping it short, but sweet.

She fluttered her eyelashes as she drew back. 'Why thank you, Rhett. My naked bum is now safe from unwanted attention.'

But as her hand dropped from his face, he snagged her wrist, and the light in his eyes darkened. 'How about I give it some wanted attention? Back here. Tonight?'

Even though she'd prepared herself for the request, her

breathing slowed, her heart thumping harder against her ribs as his thumb stroked her wrist. 'We can't, Carter. This isn't going to happen again.'

'That's a shame. When we both enjoy it so much.'

She could hardly argue with that, given that her pulse was currently doing the foxtrot under his stroking thumb.

His eyebrow lifted. 'Do you have a reason, or am I gonna have to guess what it is?'

She pulled her wrist free, and gripped the strap of her bag. 'I just don't want this turning into a…a…' *What? 'A thing.'*

'A thing, huh?' He ducked his head, and ran a finger across his bottom lip, as if considering her response, but she could see he was struggling to suppress a grin. 'You're gonna have to tell me why a *thing* would be a problem.' His eyes lit with amusement. 'Because I've gotta tell you, I think we've already got a thing going here. It certainly felt like a hell of a thing last night.'

She clamped down on her temper, because with temper came heat, and she knew he'd exploit that straight away. 'A *thing* would be a problem,' she said patiently, 'because a thing can so easily turn into a fling.'

'O-kay.' He nodded sagely. 'And a fling is bad because…?' He gestured with his hand as if encouraging her to continue.

'You're not taking this seriously.' There was a limit to how patient she could be when he was deliberately taking the Mickey.

'Ya think?' He took her hand, linked his fingers through hers—that aggravating grin still firmly in place. 'That's because you're taking it way *too* seriously, Gina. All we're talking about here is great sex.' His thumb did that sizzling thing again, pressing into the palm of her hand. He gave her a little tug and kissed her. The touch of his lips oddly tender, behind the usual heat. 'There's no need to get your new panties in a twist. Okay, sugar?'

'Carter! You…' She huffed out a laugh. The cheeky comment and the tempting kiss making her temper dissolve into something liquid and warm.

Good heavens, the man really was dangerous. If she couldn't even stay mad at him when she needed to.

She slapped a hand on his chest, to wrench herself away from that handsome face, those tempting lips, and the wicked promise in his eyes. 'I have to shoot. Thanks for the panties.'

He let her go, and remained silent as she rushed to the door, far too aware of the soft lace stretching over her moist sex. But as she left the room without risking a backward glance she knew she hadn't finished their fling—or thing, or whatever the heck it was—quite as quickly or cleanly or concisely as she had intended.

And that was a definite worry.

Much more of a worry, though, was the intoxicating spurt of endorphins that accompanied the thought.

CHAPTER SEVEN

GINA STEPPED OFF the cobblestone street into the exclusive bridal boutique nestled under the Manhattan Bridge Overpass. Rails full of fanciful white and ivory dresses crowded the front of the shop, but she could already hear the musical lilt of female laughter from the back of the store. Reese appeared in her usual pristine combo of skinny designer jeans and a chic fitted blouse, her hair pinned up in an unfussy chignon and with a champagne flute full of what Gina hoped was something alcoholic in her hand.

'Late as usual. Where have you been? The start time was eleven a.m. prompt, not—' she shot a look at the gold watch on her wrist '—quarter to twelve.'

Gina opened her mouth to deliver the white lie she'd been working on during the cab ride to the hip-and-happening Brooklyn neighbourhood when Reese simply waved her hand and passed her the flute. 'Don't bother, I can take a wild guess. I just hope he was worth it.'

'Good to know I'm that transparent,' Gina remarked dryly, taking a healthy sip of the fruity mimosa to cover the tremor in her fingers and project her usual cool. Reese didn't know about her new leaf, so she'd probably just assume last night had been another of her casual hook-ups. Which of course it was, she corrected herself smoothly. Completely casual.

Reese grinned and looped her arm through Gina's to lead

her to the back of the shop. 'I know a well-screwed look when I see one.'

Gina spluttered, the second sip hitting her larynx. Was it *that* obvious?

'Why, Gina?' Reese stopped to study her.

Heat leached into Gina's cheeks.

'That's not a blush, is it? Have we slipped into an alternative reality?'

'Hardly. I just didn't get a lot of sleep last night—as you so correctly assumed.' Gina pressed the cool glass to her cheeks to get the stupid blush under control as they entered a small, intimate salon.

The remains of bagels, take-out coffee mugs and a fruit plate littered the low table in the centre of the room beside a half-full bottle of champagne and a large jug of iced orange juice.

'Gina, you're here!' Cassie sent a slightly desperate smile from her seat on one of the soft leather sofas that framed the table. 'Nearly an hour late, as usual.' She frowned. 'I wonder if you can have a genetic compulsion to inefficient time-keeping?' Dressed in her geek's uniform of battered jeans and a shapeless T with the proclamation 'Soil Scientists Know All the Dirt' printed on it in bold pink lettering, she had that rabbit-in-the-headlights look she always got when forced to make fashion choices.

'There you go, Reese,' Gina chimed in, grateful for the change of subject. 'It's a genetic compulsion. I can't help being late.'

'Given what you were up to last night,' Reese chirped in, dragging the subject back to where Gina didn't want it, 'inefficient time-keeping's not your only genetic compulsion.'

'Hey, Gina.' Marnie caught her gaze in one of the salon's mirrored walls as she modelled a stunning off-the-shoulder chiffon gown for Reese's petite friend Amber—who looked like an industrious pixie buzzing around Marnie with a row of pins held between pursed lips. Amber threw a quick wave of greeting, which Gina returned, before getting back to the business of popping the pins into the gown's hem. The deep aquamarine of the material intensified the blue of Marnie's eyes—and gave Gina an uncomfortable memory flash of another penetrating gaze. She broke eye contact and shrugged off the guilt.

None of her friends would ever know who she'd been with last night. Least of all Marnie. It had been a one-off. A steamy swansong to that night ten years ago brought on by chemistry and curiosity. Well, they'd both satisfied that curiosity now. Maybe not completely satisfied it, because the chemistry was still super hot, but satisfied it enough. So there would be no need for a replay and nothing to feel guilty about.

Reese leaned in and whispered theatrically, 'I'll want the full story on your coffee morning later. But Marnie says you booked an awesome venue for you know what.'

Gina gulped down the last of the mimosa and sent Reese a bland stare. 'Be aware, I still haven't forgiven you for setting me and Marnie up with your little disappearing act.'

Reese's grin only widened. 'What are you talking about?' she said, not even attempting to look innocent. 'I was unavoidably detained.'

'Where exactly? In Mason's boudoir?'

'Possibly.' Reese wiggled her eyebrows, the grin taking on a cheeky quality.

'What are you two whispering about?' Cassie came over to join them, popping a piece of melon in her mouth.

'Mason's bondage techniques,' Gina said dryly. 'What else?'

Cassie rolled her eyes, comically. 'What? *Again?*'

Reese laughed. 'Excuse me, but who was it who was just regaling us with Tuck's amazing powers of recuperation?'

Cassie frowned, nonplussed. 'I was simply trying to con-tribute to the apocryphal data being accrued. I never men-tioned Tuck's name.'

Reese patted Cassie's cheek with loving condescension. 'Let's just say we all made an informed decision about who your subject matter was based on the factual data you logged in the discussion. And the fact that my cousin is the only guy you're sleeping with now and for ever. Unlike our friend Gina.' She sent a sly glance Gina's way. 'Maybe you'd like to contribute to Cassie's research on the performance capacity of the adult American male with a contribution of recorded data from last night's mystery man? Assuming of course he was another Yank.'

'Actually, he's not a...' Gina cut off the wry quip—before she blurted out far too much recordable data about her mys-tery man, who'd once explained to her on a moonlit night in Hillbrook that calling a Southerner a Yankee ranked right up in the league table of unforgivable national slurs with calling an Irishman English.

'So not a Yank?' Reese's brows rose with interest. 'How very cosmopolitan of you.'

'Why don't those who are getting regular sex stop boast-ing about it?' Marnie cut in from across the room. 'So Amber can get the rest of these glorious bridesmaids' gowns fitted and we can get down to the important business of finishing the mimosas.'

'I'll second that.' Gina rushed to re-direct the conversation, again, and avoid any more out-of-character blushes. 'Amber, you've outdone yourself. That design is absolutely stunning. And the colour looks fabulous on you, Marnie.'

'Thanks, that's real sweet of you.' Marnie nodded, ac-knowledging the compliment, the smile on her face less re-served than their last meeting. 'It's like wearing a work of art.'

Amber smiled brightly as she stood to stretch her back and

admire her own handiwork. 'Reese and I wanted a design that would flatter you all without being too overblown. I've done yours in emerald. You want to strip off and I'll go get it?'

'Absolutely,' Gina replied, sending up a silent prayer of thanks for Carter's knicker gift as she stripped down to her underwear—and the conversation lapsed into a debate about styles and fabrics and colours, and the brilliance of Amber's designs, and sashayed comfortably away from the subject of her mystery man.

She didn't miss the irony though as the morning wore on in companionable girl talk, the five women enjoying some serious bonding time together in preparation for Reese's big day at the end of next month, and—while Cassie was firmly out-of-earshot in the dressing room forced to try on some push-up bras—in the whispered preparations for Cassie's impromptu wedding to Tuck. Who would have predicted ten years ago the once hopelessly romantic Marnie would be the only one of the Awesome Foursome—apart from her—not to find the man of her dreams?

Gina wondered if Marnie still harboured any of those fanciful hopes about finding Mr Right—that she had once sneered at.

It was pretty ironic that the only wobble she'd ever had in that regard had been Marnie's big brother. After ten years and the roller coaster she'd been forced to ride after that long ago summer, she doubted she would make that mistake again—but given her history with Carter, steering clear of him for the rest of the week until he was safely back in Savannah made sense. What made it imperative though was a morning spent observing Amber and Reese and Cassie. Because the evidence of how far gone the three of them were over the men in their lives was both irrefutable, and pretty damn scary.

Take Amber and her insane decision to sublet her apartment above the shop and move into Parker's place located near his job in the fifty-seventh precinct—thus giving herself an hour-long commute into work every day—just because her taciturn cop had said he'd rather be shot in the head than live above a bridal boutique. Or Reese and her equally insane decision to set up a non-profit organisation with Mason to utilise the skills of military veterans in disaster zones. Second Chance, First Response sounded like a worthwhile concept, but also like a lot of hard work, something she wasn't convinced Reese had considered before she'd committed to the project. Because it was pretty obvious when Reese had explained how tough it was for veterans to adjust to civilian life, using Mason's ongoing struggle since his honourable discharge as an example, that Reese had made the decision to commit to the non-profit with her heart first and her head a distant second.

But by far the biggest shock of the morning had been the change in Cassie—grounded, academically brilliant, IQ-off-the-charts Cassie—the person Gina had always relied upon to give her a no-nonsense, pragmatic perspective on her own sometimes volatile emotions. Cassie had actually emitted something that sounded suspiciously like a giggle when talking about her upcoming wedding. Since when had her friend become a giggler? What else could have caused that but the Tuck Effect?

So now she had conclusive proof. Great sex could lead to dementia. And while she found it unbearably sweet that Reese, and Amber, and Cassie had found men who they were prepared to change their lives for, risking getting a dose of that dementia wasn't for Gina. She was a single girl, who loved living her life solo. Men were great in small doses, especially when you needed that special flesh-on-flesh endorphin fix, but they were not an option for the long haul. Not for her.

She didn't want to compromise her life, to adjust her dreams, to shrink her own ambitions to fit somebody else's.

And while Carter had certainly proved he could hit her happy buttons with a great deal more style and panache than any other guy she'd ever dated, he had also been the only man ever to come close to making her want more than great sex and stimulating small talk. And while that had happened a long time ago, in a galaxy far, far away—she wasn't interested in a return journey.

'Hey, earth to Gina?' Cassie waved a hand in front of her face.

Gina's head jerked, making her bobble the mimosa she'd forgotten she had in her hand. She saved it in the nick of time from splattering her dress.

'Sorry, I didn't mean to startle you, but Amber was asking if you had a preference for gold or silver trim on your gown.'

'Oh, right, yes, I think silver,' she said off the top of her head, trying to remember what colour her gown was, while four pairs of eyes looked at her quizzically.

'Where were you?' Cassie asked, a small frown on her brow. 'You looked several light years away.'

'Nowhere in particular.'

'I think I can take a wild guess.' Reese refilled her glass. 'You weren't somewhere in the vicinity of the Mystery Studmuffin, were you?'

'The mystery what?' Marnie asked.

Damn. She should have been paying attention to the conversation instead of wasting time thinking about the mystery studmuffin she was never going to see again.

Heat seared Gina's neck as Reese toasted her with her flute.

'Bingo.' Reese winked at Marnie. 'The Mystery Studmuffin is the hot guy Gina was with last night—and this morning while she was supposed to be with us. All we know about him so far is that he isn't an American, he's a hot enough date to give Gina a genetic compulsion to terrible time-keeping...'

'Her date can't have caused it if it's a genetic compulsion, no matter how hot he is,' Cassie corrected her.

'Point taken...' Reese continued, undaunted. 'But he is hot enough to make the Unflappable Miss Carrington blush. So on a hotness scale of one to ten, I'm guessing the Mystery Studmuffin goes all the way to eleven.'

Marnie and Amber both laughed, while the blush climbed into Gina's cheeks.

'So who is he?' Reese teased. 'Enquiring minds want to know every intimate detail.'

'Well, enquiring minds can mind their own business,' Gina replied, pretty sure the blush was about to reach her hairline. 'Unlike you lot, I'm not into shag and share.'

'Since when?' Reese looked genuinely surprised.

'Since I became a grown-up.' She slapped her glass down on the table, the hot ball of resentment in her stomach only intensifying the guilty heat now scalding her scalp. 'And stopped banging every guy that took my fancy. Not that anyone here would believe that of Gina the Unflappable Whore.'

Reese's teasing smile disappeared as her jaw went slack, while the other women's eyes popped to the size of dinner plates.

'Gina, I'm sorry, I was only messing with you,' Reese murmured, looking thoroughly crestfallen.

Gina hoisted her purse off the floor and stood. 'I should go,' she said stiffly, wanting to apologise for the petulant outburst, but not sure how to do it without making things worse. 'I'm tired and it's making me more of a bitch than usual.'

Reese jumped up to press a hand to her arm. 'Please, Gina, don't go. I feel awful. No one thinks you're a whore.'

Gina caught Marnie's eye, and the other woman blinked, her face ashen, clearly shaken by the mention of the word that had once torn them all apart.

You would though, if you knew who I was really with last night.

She patted Reese's fingers, then gently disengaged them from her arm. 'Really it's okay. I was being ridiculously over-sensitive. And I really do need to crash. I'll speak to you in the week about...' she lowered her voice to a whisper so only Reese could hear '...you know whose surprise party.'

'All right, if you're sure.'

'Sure, I'm sure.' She bade goodbye to the others and left, escaping before their gestures of support and concern could make her do something dopey, like bursting into tears.

It wasn't until she was in the cab home, bouncing across the cobblestoned street past Brooklyn Park, and she'd got the foolish urge to cry under lockdown, that she began to wonder where exactly the hot ball of resentment had come from that had caused her to end an immensely enjoyable morning of BFF bonding on such a sour note. And once she'd digested the only possible answer to that question, she then had to ask herself why she should resent what Reese and Cassie and Amber had—when she'd decided years ago that she would never want the same thing for herself.

Once back at the minute loft apartment she was struggling to pay the rent on in Brooklyn's funky Red Hook district, Gina stripped off her clothes, took another hot shower and crashed straight into the fanciful iron-framed double bed she'd crammed into the loft's bedroom. Given that she was now at the grand old age of twenty-nine and somewhat out of practice, clearly her all-nighter with Carter had taken a physical toll that had had emotional repercussions. But once she'd caught up on her sleep, she'd be herself again—and everything would snap back into sharp, vivid focus.

Several hours later, after a fitful nap that had been filled with far too many erotic dreams featuring the Mystery Studmuffin who should not be named, the door buzzer sounded. She crawled out of bed, her pulse pounding into her throat and a few other more intimate parts of her anatomy—until she spied Cassie's face through the peephole. The dip in her stomach had nothing whatsoever to do with disappointment, she decided as she yanked open the heavy security door.

'Gina, you look wasted,' Cassie announced as she stepped into the flat with a garment bag hooked over her shoulder. 'Maybe you're coming down with flu.'

If only.

'No, I have the constitution of an ox. I'm just exhausted.'

Cassie sent her a bland look, but fortunately didn't probe. 'Amber asked me to drop this off for you.' She handed her the garment bag, which had the white logo of Amber's Bridal emblazoned across it. 'She told me to tell you she's done the necessary adjustments, but she needs you to try it on and send it back, just to make sure the fit's good before she starts adding the other bits.'

'Thanks for bringing it over.' Gina laid the bag over the back of her sofa. 'I'm sorry you had to come all this way. I should have stuck around, shouldn't I?'

Cassie simply said, 'Are you asking me a question? Because I know absolutely nothing about the etiquette of bridal fittings.'

Gina smiled at the clueless comment. 'How about a coffee for your trouble?'

'Only if you're sure you don't want to get back to your nap?'

'Positive,' Gina replied, keen to avoid returning to her nap, which was causing more problems than it solved.

To her great relief Cassie agreed to stay and Gina set about making the coffee.

'Is everything okay? You seem a little shaky.' The cautious comment had Gina's hand halting as it ladled coffee into the

French press. Cassie wasn't the most intuitive person in the world, so it had to be really obvious.

'Yes, of course,' she said, determined to make it so as she started ladling again. 'Why wouldn't it be?'

'You totally overreacted to Reese's teasing,' Cassie replied with her customary bluntness. 'Which made me wonder if something bad happened last night.'

Gina smoothed her palms down her robe, touched by Cassie's concern. She filled the French press with boiling water and faced her friend. 'And there I was thinking I had my poker face on.'

'I would strongly suggest you don't enter any poker tournaments, then—you wouldn't make much money.'

Gina sent Cassie a weak smile. 'Don't worry, Cass, nothing bad happened. It was all good.' *Way too good, really.*

'Was it Marnie's brother?' Cassie asked, her expression direct and totally non-judgmental. 'The guy you were with last night?'

The blush fired up Gina's neck as she opened her mouth to deny it—but her mind went completely blank, and the manufactured outrage, the clever evasions, the bald-faced lie she wanted to tell got trapped in her throat somewhere in the region of her Adam's apple. Until all she could manage to choke out on a panicked whisper was: 'How did you know?'

'It was obvious once I'd analysed the available data.' Cassie stirred sugar into her coffee, apparently unfazed by the admission of guilt.

'Which was?'

Cassie shrugged and sipped. 'Marnie took a call from him just before you arrived, and arranged to meet him at The Standard Hotel for lunch on Tuesday, so I knew he was in town.' Cassie placed her mug on the counter with calm deliberation. 'And the only other time I've seen you blush like that is the morning after you slept with him the first time. Well, until right this minute, that is.'

'Terrific.' Gina's teeth ground together as the heat scalded her ears. 'Did you share your brilliant powers of deduction with anyone else?'

'No.' A tiny frown bisected Cassie's brow as Gina's breath gushed out and the knots in her shoulders loosened a little. 'But why would that be bad?' Cassie asked, giving a slow owlish blink—which Gina knew meant she was trying to process something particularly complex.

'Because I don't want Reese and Marnie to know.' She ruthlessly resisted the urge to say 'Duh'. It wasn't Cassie's fault she'd figured out the truth, or that she was so clueless about the dynamics of female friendships.

'Why don't you want them to know?'

Oh, for Pete's sake.

'Because I screwed up this friendship once before by screwing Marnie's brother—and I don't want to do it again.'

'But you did screw him again, so whether they know or not is sort of academic, isn't it?'

'Yes, but…' Gina stammered to a halt, totally lost for words in the face of Cassie's objective reasoning. 'I can't believe I've done this again. It's like I've got a genetic compulsion to screw up this friendship.'

'Not necessarily,' Cassie said, taking the statement literally as always. 'To determine that you'd have to examine the cause and effect.'

'The…. Well, it wasn't planned, if that's what you're asking.' Because who knew what the heck Cassie was on about now? 'I went to his hotel to apologise to him.'

'What for?' Cassie cut in, looking shocked for the first time.

'For the failure of his marriage.'

'How was that your fault?'

'Apparently it wasn't,' Gina added, suddenly keen to end this topic of conversation. Because the apology excuse for seeing Carter again was sounding less and less valid, even to her. 'Do you want to hear the rest or not?'

Cassie's eyebrows rose fractionally at the tone. 'Yes.'

'Fine, well, then, after he'd told me his divorce was none of my concern, we had a few drinks, one thing led to another and before I knew it we were tearing each other's clothes off in his very nice corner suite overlooking the Hudson.' She sighed. 'The views really are spectacular from that hotel, by the way.'

'What view are we talking about?' Cassie said, so dryly Gina choked out a laugh, the burden of guilt lifting for the first time since her meltdown at the salon.

'It's not funny,' she replied. 'It's disastrous. I know that. But the good news is, it won't happen again. I told him in no uncertain terms this morning that we'd made a mistake.' Well, the terms hadn't been that uncertain, but still.

'How was it?' Cassie asked.

'How was what?'

'The mistake?'

'You mean the sex?'

Cassie nodded.

'Honestly?'

Another nod.

'Fabulous.' Why lie about it? 'As I believe I mentioned ten years ago, the man was a gifted amateur. He's more than lived up to that early promise.' Which she was beginning to realise only made the mistake of sleeping with him all the more enormous—because her ability to conjure up an image of him naked and ready with complete clarity was not helping.

'Maybe that explains it, then,' Cassie mused.

'Explains what?'

'Why you slept with him, despite your misgivings. Studies

have shown the release of endorphins triggered by orgasm—which for the purposes of this discussion we'll call fabulous sex—can impair your cognitive skills. They certainly impaired mine when I had sex with Tuck the first time. And the second. And the…'

'I get the picture,' Gina muttered. Trust Cassie to come up with a scientific solution—that made perfect sense to her and no sense in the real world. 'Cass, what you and Tuck have is not the same as what Carter and I have. Frankly, having sex with Carter could turn me into Dumbo, but all it would ultimately prove is that Marnie was right about me all along.'

Cassie gave a pensive hum. 'Are you sure you're giving Marnie enough credit? Why don't you ask her whether she cares about you and Carter getting back together.'

Gina choked on her coffee. 'Are you on crack or something?' she whispered furiously. 'Carter and I are *not* back together, because we never were together. This isn't a relationship. It's one night of madness.'

'Two now, actually.'

'All right, two,' Gina conceded. Trust Cassie to be pedantic about the maths. 'But now it's over.' Of that much she was certain.

'Did you tell him about the baby?'

The blood drained out of Gina's face and slammed into her heart. 'No, of course not. Why would I?'

'I just thought…' Cassie began. 'He's not married any more—so why would you need to keep it a secret still?'

'Because it's ancient history. Because there would be no point in telling him all these years after the fact.' She coughed, trying to lower her voice, which had become a little shrill in the face of Cassie's passive-aggressive interrogation techniques. 'And anyway it was never a baby. It was a miscarriage.' And she'd spent a great deal of time, not to mention money, making herself believe that.

It had taken her years to repair the damage she'd done to her sense of self-worth and self-esteem. And even longer to become a more stable, sorted person—a person who could actually look at herself in the mirror every morning and like what she saw. She'd had to get over the insecurities of her childhood, the recklessness of her adolescence and the horror of what had happened when she'd returned to England with Carter's child growing inside her womb, harbouring some idiotic notion that she'd fallen in love with a man who was totally unattainable.

But none of that had really had anything to do with Carter. She'd latched onto him, because he'd listened to her that night, he'd been sensitive and sweet and the few things he'd told her about his father had made her think they might be kindred spirits. But the truth was, he'd just been the catalyst.

Unfortunately, last night proved that she still had a ways to go before she could rely on herself to resist all temptations. But last night had no real bearing on her past. It had been nothing more than a biological urge. An irresistible biological urge. Which meant the decision not to see Carter again, and stir up any more irresistible biological urges, was the mature choice. And if Cassie would just back off, and stop making ridiculous suggestions, she might actually be able to embrace it.

'Okay, if you say so,' Cassie interrupted her panicked revelry, her calm grey eyes fixed on Gina's face.

'I do say so, because it's the truth.'

Cassie looked doubtful—what she wasn't saying hanging in the air between them, like a huge pulsing neon sign. And Gina knew exactly what the sign said.

You're in denial.

She could see Cassie believed it wasn't panic over screwing up her relationship with her friends that had Gina steering clear of Carter now. It was all the messy, unfinished business between the two of them that she didn't want to confront.

And it was hardly surprising Cassie had that misconception.

Because during those months after Gina had left Hillbrook—when she'd discovered the pregnancy and a few crucial months later lost the baby—Reese and Cassie had been there to help her pick up the pieces, at the end of a transatlantic phone line. They'd let Gina rant and rave, and cry and carry on and finally come to terms with her loss and her grief, but there had been one thing her two best friends had disagreed with her about. They both felt Gina should have contacted Carter. That he should have been forced to share some of the emotional burden, because he had been as responsible as Gina for that short, helpless little life.

Gina placed her fingers on Cassie's arm and squeezed. 'It's not what you think, Cass. Honestly. I'm not a basketcase any more. I'm all grown up. I got over it. I couldn't be more different from that girl. And Carter's a completely different guy too. Give or take the odd super power in the sack,' she added wryly.

Cassie sent her a tentative smile. 'Maybe you're right.'

'I know I am.'

'But if that's the case, it does pose another question.'

'Which is?'

'If all the variables have changed, and Reese and Marnie never need to know about this—what's preventing you from availing yourself of Carter's super powers again?'

CHAPTER EIGHT

CASSIOPEIA BARCLAY, I want to throttle you.

Gina took her eyes off the phone, punched her computer's start-up button and lobbed Carter Price's card into the wastepaper basket—for the fiftieth time in the last seven days.

The big digital clock above her kitchen counter clicked from 10:59 to 11:00 as she struggled to focus on the screen and ignore the residual hum of heat pulsing in her abdomen.

Ignore it. He's probably already on his plane to Savannah. You did it.

Why she didn't feel particularly thrilled with her powers of resistance was neither here nor there.

She dragged her gaze back to the blog she was designing for an organic farmer's community up in Westchester. It was a new commission and she'd been toying with different basic designs for two days. She punched keys, finally picking a beautiful leaf green for the background to complement the community's logo.

At last, progress.

Business had been painfully slow recently—people generally didn't think too much about social-media marketing campaigns when they were struggling to pay their bills—and she needed to make an impact with this commission. She'd promised the co-operative at least fifty thousand unique visitors in their first three months, which meant putting together a blog package with the wow factor.... And achieving that when the majority of your subject matter was organically grown potatoes was no mean feat.

Once she'd finished the preliminary designs, she began to rough in some of the copy they'd sent her for the launch. And pretended not to notice the insistent punch of her heartbeat every time she glanced at the clock—and another minute had crawled by.

Carter leapt up the steps to the loft apartment two at a time. He had exactly an hour till check-in closed on his flight to Savannah. With a major board meeting scheduled for five this afternoon in Georgia he couldn't miss his plane. So what the hell was he doing getting his cab driver to detour to Brooklyn?

He guessed he was about to find out as he reached the second floor landing and pressed the door buzzer marked Carrington Web Designs.

If she was out, that would be all the answer he needed. He'd left it up to her to call and she hadn't—but he figured she owed him an explanation. She'd approached him, she'd made the first contact, and then she'd blown his mind in that damn hotel suite, leaving him tense and edgy and unfocused for the rest of his trip when he should have been concentrating on business.

He'd drifted off during more than one important negotiation in the last week—eventually making the trip a wash with the Chinese clients he'd been pursuing for months, who now thought he was the next best thing to a narcoleptic.

He could have happily lived the rest of his life never having stirred up this hornet's nest again. But she'd insisted on stirring it up, and then figured she could just unstir it again at her own convenience. Well, to hell with that.

He thumped on the security door, drew back his fist to

thump again, when the door swung open. And the muscles in his gut cinched into a tight knot.

It was eleven ten on a Friday morning but she looked as if she'd just rolled out of bed. Her hair fell around her shoulders in big, fluffy, unkempt waves that made him want to plunge his fingers in and ruffle it up some more. Her clear, pale skin glowed, scrubbed clean without the benefit of the carefully applied make-up she usually wore, while the loose robe gave him a painful glimpse of a lacy camisole barely covering firm breasts.

'Carter, what the…? You're supposed to be in Savannah!'

She tightened the tie on her robe, and her breasts plumped up, threatening to spill out of the lace altogether. The knot in his gut sank lower, loosening muscles that had been too tight for days.

He dragged his gaze away from her cleavage—and suddenly knew the answer.

This wasn't over, not till he said so. Not this time. But from now on he was playing the game on his terms. Not hers. And that meant getting the upper hand right from the get-go.

'I'm on my way to La Guardia now, but I've got a proposition for you that I wanted to deliver in person.'

'What proposition?'

He stroked a finger down her cheek, enjoying the way her lips parted and a sob of breath came out.

She was no more immune than he was to this *thing*. And it was a *thing*, however you wanted to call it.

'I want you to come to Savannah for a couple of weeks.'

She blinked, the movement slow and tremulous, as if she were trying to process the invitation. 'I can't do that, Carter. We're not kids any more and I don't think…'

He pressed his finger to her lips, silencing the protest. 'Now don't go getting your panties in a twist again—that's not the kind of proposition I'm talking about.'

'Oh?'

He felt the surge of satisfaction at the catch of disappointment in her voice and the pucker of confusion on her brow.

You're not the only one who can play hard ball, sugar.

'As great as it was on Friday night, this is a business proposition.' *Mostly.*

'What kind of business proposition?'

The pucker got more pronounced, but he could see the spark of interest lurking behind the caution.

'I've been giving it some thought.' At least ten seconds anyway. 'And I'd like to commission you to work on a social-media campaign for the mill. We're expanding into a number of new markets and we need to up our profile—social media is a way to do that without breaking the bank.'

'That's… Really?'

'Yeah, really, at the moment we only have a website—which we'll need you to redesign—but we're also looking to build a more comprehensive strategy across all the appropriate social-media platforms.'

'That's an excellent idea—over two billion people use the web. But I should warn you that it doesn't necessarily translate into sales straight away. The idea is to…' She stopped suddenly, pushed the door open, the enthusiasm sparking in her eyes almost making him feel guilty. But then he remembered it was a real job, he'd got the funding approved by the board months ago—and he got the final say on who to hire, so he could hire her if he wanted. 'Why don't you come in? We can discuss it further.' She glanced at her clothing. 'I'll get dressed and we can…'

'No need to get dressed on my account.' He let his gaze drift down the shorty robe past long, toned legs to bare feet, and toes painted cotton-candy pink. And imagined himself nibbling on that cute little pinkie. He let the innuendo heat the air, before returning his gaze to her face. Her breathing had speeded up, making her cleavage rise and fall against the confining lace. 'I can't stop to discuss it now. I've got a plane to catch. That's why I need you to come to Savannah.'

'But I don't have to be in Georgia. Everything can be done online and we can correspond via email.'

He smiled—he'd definitely heard the disappointment that time. And the way her voice had lowered to the throaty purr that signalled her arousal.

'I want you to see the mill, talk to the folks that work there, get a clear picture of who we are and what we do.' Damned if he hadn't almost convinced himself by the time he'd finished outlining all the elements of the operation he wanted her to get acquainted with.

'Well, I suppose…'

He leant in and pressed a quick perfunctory kiss to her lips, heard her sharp intake of breath. 'Great, that's all settled. I'll get my PA to negotiate a contract and email flight details. Can you make it down early next week?'

'If you're sure you need me to be there.'

'I'm sure.'

'Then I guess that settles it.'

He stepped back, cursing the fact that he'd be riding an erection all the way to the airport as his lungs filled with the sunny scent of her hair. He let his gaze wander over her figure. 'As much as I like that get-up, you might want to pack a few more clothes. But keep them light—it's hot and sticky in Savannah at this time of year.' And even though his house in the city's Victorian Historic District was well air-conditioned, he had a feeling it was going to be even hotter and stickier there once she was sleeping down the hall.

The smile she sent him made him suspect she wasn't going to play all that hard to get. But then neither was he. 'Okay.'

'See you later.' He nodded, the words more than a little husky.

But as he turned to go she touched his arm. 'Just a second, Carter. Did you speak to Marnie this week?'

'Sure, we had lunch on Tuesday.' The usual strained, stilted affair.

'And you didn't tell her about us? About Friday night?'

'I said I wouldn't,' he replied, not sure where the irritation came from. It wasn't as if he and Marnie were bosom buddies. Even though their mama had raised her never to say it, he knew Marnie thought he was a womanising jerk. He knew that and he accepted it—it was part of the penance he paid for that night—and frankly Marnie's bad opinion had been the least of his worries as he watched his marriage disintegrate.

Since the divorce and their mother's death, Marnie had kept her distance, pursuing a career in New York that he knew very little about—and making caustic comments on the few occasions they met about his being the playboy of the western world. He didn't bother to deny it, because he didn't need her approval—and he hadn't exactly been a monk. But he also didn't plan to give Marnie more ammunition, so the last thing he'd be likely to do was mention to his sister that he'd had an all-nighter with Gina again. But the spurt of annoyance was there none the less. Not just because Gina had doubted his word, but because she seemed so damned determined to keep their *thing* a secret. He didn't like secrets, because they could come back and bite you on the butt.

'Could I ask you to keep quiet about this arrangement too?' she said.

'Sure, if that's the way you want it.' He shrugged, trying not to care. 'Marnie doesn't get involved in mill business, she just helps herself to the company's equity,' he said, the statement coming out with more bitterness than he'd intended when he saw Gina frown.

'If you say so,' she murmured and the prickle of irritation became a definite stab. 'I'll see you in a few days.'

'Yeah.' He waved her goodbye and jogged down the stairs, conceding that a few days seemed like a mighty long time.

Gina slammed the door and leaned against it, her diamond-hard nipples making the silk of her camisole feel like sandpaper.

Way to go, Gina. After going cold turkey for a whole week, your drug of choice appears and you resist temptation for precisely ten seconds.

She rolled her eyes and squeezed her thighs together to stop the insistent ache that had settled there as soon as she'd encountered Carter Price standing on her doorstep. His dark hair furrowed into rows and those cobalt eyes even bluer than usual.

She pursed her lips.

Carter wouldn't have offered her this commission unless he thought she would do a competent job—his business was far too important to him for that—but the lingering sizzle where his mouth had touched hers in that casual but proprietary kiss told a slightly different story. That the decision to offer her this opportunity might not be entirely based on the glowing testimonials on her website.

As an independent working woman with a fledgling business she was proud of, she should be outraged.

She padded across the apartment to the bathroom and shrugged out of her robe. Tossing the camisole over her head, she stepped into the enamel bath and switched the dial on the shower unit to scalding.

Unfortunately, though, she couldn't quite muster the required indignation because her decision to accept Carter's offer had had more to do with the intoxicating pheromones he released without even trying—which had caused every one of the synapses in her brain to fuse in unison the second she saw him—than it did with the fabulous opportunity this commission would offer her struggling business.

As the water pounded down, and she soaped her over-sensitive breasts with rather more vigour than was entirely necessary, she could almost hear Cassie's dry Aussie accent saying: 'I told you endorphins are addictive.'

—

CHAPTER NINE

GINA DABBED AT the sheen of sweat on her brow as she sat in the airy outer office of the Price Paper Mill. A large picture window looked down on the factory floor, where the mill's mostly recycled paper products were manufactured, giving her a slight flutter of vertigo to go with her nerves.

She gripped her laptop bag as Carter's young but efficient PA Bella Delmarr smiled benignly at her from behind a neat white desk.

'Mr Price will be along shortly, Miz Carrington. Would you like some iced tea or a soda while you wait?'

'No, I'm fine,' she replied, not sure she'd be able to swallow without choking, given her jumpy stomach. Which was ridiculous. Why was she so apprehensive about seeing him?

She'd done her homework in the last three days, putting together a preliminary package for him to review—which included projections for the different social media platforms, what they could hope to achieve, some blog designs, website analytics and ideas for possible marketing campaigns to enhance the company's profile. Unfortunately, while doing all that, she'd discovered that the Price family's paper mill had grown from a virtually bankrupt business when Carter had stepped into the CEO's shoes after his father's death into a huge multinational enterprise cleverly cornering the market in the South in recycled products. All of which made Carter's offer of a commission not just a great opportunity, but easily the best she'd ever had.

She could not afford to mess this up—which meant she could not afford to mess with Carter. And while that was extremely disappointing on a number of levels, by far her biggest concern was getting her libido—and Carter—to co-operate. Because she had a feeling his agenda might not be quite so professional—and saying no to him had never been one of her strong suits.

She smoothed damp palms down the linen trousers she'd worn to ward off the intense humidity—only to have the sweat pop back out onto her top lip as the man himself walked through the adjoining door from his office.

'Gina, you made it.'

She got out of her chair and shook the hand he offered. The familiar shot of adrenaline raced up her arm at the touch of his cool dry fingers. 'Yes, I have some projections for you to look at.' She lifted her laptop.

'Great, why don't you leave that with Bella?' He nodded to his PA. 'I'll give you the tour first and then we can take a look.'

She passed the laptop over, disconcerted by the intense cobalt gaze that wandered over her outfit, contradicting the businesslike tone.

'I hope you're not too hot.' He placed a wide palm on the base of her spine, steering her to the stairwell that led to the factory floor. 'Humidity hit ninety per cent today—which is manageable for a native, but let me know if you're gonna wilt and we'll take a break.'

It wasn't the humidity that was likely to make her wilt, she thought, as his palm rubbed before it dropped away, sending tendrils of heat shooting up her spine through the silk of her blouse.

'Ninety per cent is more than I'd bargained for,' she re-

plied as they left the air-conditioned stairwell and hit a wall
of heat. It was like walking into a steam room, the wet, humid
warmth slapping into them with the force of a wave. 'When
you said hot and sticky, I wasn't expecting the Seventh Circle
of Hell,' she added, deciding that talking about the weather
was probably the safest bet.

He rolled up his shirt sleeves, and she could see the glow
of sweat on his brow beneath his hairline. Her mouth dried
as she registered the sudden urge to run her tongue across his
forehead and lick off the salty beads of moisture. The way
she'd done on that hot summer night in Hillbrook.

*Down, girl. Remember: businesslike, professional, fo-
cused, at all times. You're not going to screw up your big
break for an endorphin fix. This is your new leaf talking.*

His sensual lips curved into an easy smile that had 'fo-
cused' falling by the wayside straight away. 'Ninety per cent
is nothing,' he said in that lazy Southern drawl that never
failed to reverberate in her abdomen. 'Forecast is for it to
get a whole lot hotter over the next couple of weeks.' The
wicked glint in those heavy-lidded eyes made it fairly obvious this was not a conversation about the weather any more.
'You think you can handle the heat?'

'Absolutely,' she lied.

The rest of the afternoon passed in a haze of information as he
showed her round the whole operation, displaying a hands-on
knowledge of the production process—and his employees—
that surprised and intrigued her.

From the little Marnie had let slip about her brother and
what Gina had discovered on the Internet, she'd assumed
Carter Price CEO would be as dominant and cynical as Carter
Price Lover Man.

But after taking the tour of his factory, she'd discovered
the sheep in wolf's clothing.

She'd thought he would focus on the big picture, the business side of his business—and leave the nitty-gritty of production and supply to his minions. And she hadn't expected him to know every one of his employees by their first names—right down to the pimply faced teenager who swept the loading bay. Or to know enough about their lives to ask after new babies, or recent marriages, or Great-Aunt Merilou's bursitis. But Carter Price had known about all of those things, chatting in a relaxed, comfortable way that suggested these people weren't his minions, they were his friends. And it was also obvious they all felt the same way about Carter—talking to him with easy smiles on their faces and affection as well as admiration in their eyes.

Of course, the mill was an essential part of the local economy and Carter had saved it from going under, so it was no surprise his employees were grateful to him. But she sensed something more going on, a sort of proprietary interest, almost as if these people had the status of family as well as friends, which explained the reserved Southern manners and considered glances she'd received when he introduced her—as if they were sizing her up. She dismissed the prickle of unease, remembering that she was a professional, here on professional business, even if he did insist on touching her arm and smiling confidentially at her, in front of his 'people'.

But despite her best intentions, by the time they had settled into Carter's low-riding convertible and were bombing along a country road flanked by the ubiquitous kudzu vines that swallowed most of the landscape en route to Savannah, Gina had to admit she was feeling more than a little dazed trying to assimilate everything she'd learned.

She stole a glance at the man beside her and her pulse slowed, taking in the play of muscles as he shifted gears, the sculpted angle of his cheekbone in profile, and the way the wind whipped at his hair—making her fingers itch to sweep it back off that high forehead.

Rats. Seeing Carter Price in his natural habitat wasn't going to make him one single bit easier to resist.

'So what do you think?' He shouted the question across the console.

You're gorgeous.

The words echoed in her head, as they had been doing most of the afternoon. And it occurred to her she wasn't just admiring his looks any more, or his super powers in the sack, or even the sharp intelligence he'd shown during their chat in the Standard bar a week ago. While walking through his business with him, she'd got a glimpse of the boy she'd met a decade ago. The cynical player slipping away to reveal a man with warmth and intelligence—and an almost boyish pride in what he'd achieved, not just for himself and his company, but for his community. She wondered if Marnie had ever seen this side of him. Surely she couldn't have and still think so little of him?

But then families were often unpredictable. Growing up in close proximity to someone didn't automatically make you able to understand them—or even like them.

Take her own father—and her impossible relationship with him. Arthur Carrington had been a low-ranking member of the British aristocracy who'd inherited a venture capitalist firm from his own father—her father's ruthlessness in business had been legendary. He'd grabbed all he could with the arrogance of a man born into status and given very little back, not just in his professional life, but in his personal life as well. And although he'd been dead for over six years, Gina still shuddered when she thought of him and the cold, hard glint in his eyes as he'd kicked her out of his house ten years ago.

From what Marnie had said about Carter's chequered love life since his divorce, and from what she had discovered during the last few days about the phenomenal success of his business, Gina would have expected him to be cut from the same cloth, albeit with a layer of Southern charm added. But it seemed nothing could have been further from the truth. Was it possible he really wasn't that far removed from the idealistic and sincere young man she remembered at Hillbrook? Who had been striving to pull his family's business back from the brink but had been determined to do so in an ethical way?

And why did that concept only make her visit to Savannah seem that much more perilous?

'I'm impressed,' she said. 'You've built something amazing here—just like you hoped you would,' she added, the memory of the starry-eyed enthusiasm with which he'd once outlined his dreams for the mill all those years ago making her forget to be cautious. 'And you didn't have to become your father to do it.'

A small crinkle formed on his brow. 'What do you know about my father?'

'Only what you said about him that night.'

He slowed the car, shifted down a gear to observe her for several long moments. 'What did I say about him? I don't recall.'

Her heart bobbed into her throat and it occurred to her she had just strayed into forbidden territory. Why had she mentioned that night? They were so far past it now. And she would do better not to equate the man Carter was now with the boy he'd been, because that boy had had a very unpredictable effect on her. And if she wanted to maintain a professional distance, sharing intimate recollections probably wasn't the smartest way to go about it.

'I can't remember, not a lot.'

'You remember, or you wouldn't have made that comment.'

He didn't sound annoyed, but his expression was far too intense for merely curious—forcing her to give him an answer.

'I got the impression you didn't like him much....' A confidence that had instantly made them connect, because it was exactly how she had always felt about her own father.

'Did I tell you why?'

She shook her head. 'Not really.' He hadn't elaborated, even when she'd pushed and she couldn't deny the spark of curiosity even now. 'Marnie always described him as being larger than life—a force to be reckoned with. You seemed less impressed with him. That's all I remember.'

But she'd always wondered where that disillusionment had come from. Especially the next morning, when he'd woken up in her arms in her tiny bedroom in Reese's house and then shot out of her bed, the horror and regret plain on his stricken face. And all her stupid notions about some cosmic connection between them had shrivelled up inside her as he'd apologised with the stiff politeness of a puritan minister while rushing to get his clothes on—so he could escape out of the window and pretend he'd never been there when he returned to collect Marnie's stuff. Before racing back to Savannah to throw himself on the mercy of the woman he was due to marry. The woman he loved.

'I sure must have shot my mouth off that night.' He sent her a quick grin. 'You must have thought I was one hell of a sap.'

She hadn't thought he was a sap—not after she'd cut through the macho posturing and discovered a young man who'd seemed as lost and alone and confused as she was. She flinched at the stupidly romantic thought. 'You were certainly rather full of yourself,' she replied—because he had been, at first. 'And hopelessly sexist.'

He sent her a quick grin. 'Yeah, and as I recall you weren't shy about telling me. I still remember that comment about exactly how I was ruining the line of my designer points.'

He gave a rueful chuckle, but she cringed inside—knowing even then she'd been flirting with him.

'But I realise now you were simply looking out for your sister in the only way you knew how to.'

'That bad, huh?' he teased, but she couldn't bring herself to share the joke, the memory of that intense, conflicted young man and the way she'd mocked him far too vivid.

'And in complete denial about your sexual needs—which made you an irresistible challenge for a tramp like me.'

He flicked up the indicator to turn off the country lane onto a two-lane highway. 'Gina, honey, you weren't a tramp,' he said, with surprising conviction. 'You had a healthy libido and you weren't ashamed to enjoy it. Unlike me. I sincerely hope you are not still blaming yourself for what happened?' he asked, the question a little too astute for comfort.

She forced out a husky laugh. 'I've never been ashamed of enjoying sex. I think I gave you conclusive proof of that last week.'

'True enough,' he purred, the heavy-lidded look far too suggestive.

'But I certainly had a quality-control problem in my teens,' she added, steering them away from yet more forbidden territory. 'These days I make a point of not giving in to every passing fancy. Despite all evidence to the contrary last Friday night.'

He sent her a curious smile. 'I sure hope you're not suggesting I'm only a passing fancy, sugar?'

She drew in a breath. He'd given her the opening she needed. 'Actually, you're going to have to be,' she murmured, surprised at how depressed the thought made her feel. 'As your newly appointed web designer and social media strategist, I don't think we can afford a replay of Friday night. It will be too distracting.'

'Uh-huh?' he said, the curious smile twitching. He didn't seem annoyed by her comment, which was a good thing. Not so good was the fact that he seemed to find it fairly amusing.

'You ever try multitasking?' he asked, the glint in his eye deliberately provocative.

'I'm afraid so. And unfortunately I'm exceptionally bad at it.'

Damn, how could he have forgotten how forthright she was? She talked about sex without an ounce of calculation or subterfuge or fake modesty, in that clean crisp smoky British accent that arrowed straight into his crotch. After years spent handling women who figured sex could be bartered for love and marriage and happy ever after, Gina Carrington's attitude was refreshingly straightforward—and one heck of a turn-on.

Not so much of a turn-on, though, was what she was saying through those luscious lips of hers. Lips he'd wanted to feast on as soon as he'd seen her sitting in the mill's reception area looking hot and determined and aloof.

Swallowing down the groan that was threatening to rumble out of his throat, he kept his hands on the steering wheel and his gaze on the road ahead—and mulled over the problem.

What had seemed like a fairly simply seduction at the mill had become a mite more complicated. Gina's professional scruples weren't something he'd given a whole heck of a lot of thought to before offering her the commission. And now he'd seen her work, he probably should have. She was good, even better than he'd expected—the strategies she'd roughed together already exactly what they'd been looking for. Economical, well-directed and expertly designed with an originality that would make people sit up and take notice.

'I'm not gonna pretend that isn't a disappointment,' he said, keeping the lazy drawl in place as he played for time. 'But that's your prerogative.'

Just as it would be his prerogative to change her mind.

He rolled his shoulders, edging his foot off the gas pedal as the car bumped over a set of railroad tracks, and drifted into the urban sprawl of strip malls and tree-lined neighbour-hoods that marked the edge of town.

Scruples or no scruples, Gina was dead right about one thing: good sex was distracting—it was supposed to be. And when they had sex it had the potential to be nothing short of combustible.

He watched her out of the corner of his eye, the deter-mined tilt of her chin almost as beguiling as the tremble in her plump bottom lip.

Well, hell.

Gina might not be as wild and untamed as she had been as a teenager, but she still had the same volatile libido. That tiny lip tremor told him louder than words she didn't want to say no any more than he wanted to hear it. Adrenaline charged into his system, making heat pool in his lap.

While Gina might not be much good at multitasking, he happened to be a master at it. The heat surged and crested. Once upon a time, Gina had done him the favour of show-ing him that he couldn't deny his own libido. Why not use the skills he'd acquired in the years since to teach her a valu-able lesson in return—that great sex, while distracting, didn't have to be a disaster if you knew how to handle the fall-out?

He pressed his foot onto the gas, to surge past an old truck, and felt his confidence soar at the thought of the game of cat and mouse that awaited them. There would be time enough over the next few days to enjoy Gina's company, work closely together on her marketing plans—and lead her slowly but surely into temptation.

Once upon a time, she'd broken down all his inhibitions by being bold and sexy—and flirting outrageously with him—and in so doing had set him on the road to where he was now. And okay, he wasn't gonna lie, it had been a tough road during the difficult years of his marriage, rocky and painful and far far too long, but the journey had been worth it, and the destination liberating. Discovering that while he might well be his father's son, driven by the same weaknesses of the flesh, he didn't have to make the same mistakes.

So why not show Gina that she could have her cake and eat it too?

Because he had a feeling Gina's objections now had as much to do with the girl she'd been back then—who had sat in her tiny bed and accepted all the blame for his infidelity with agonising flippancy—as it did to do with the career woman she was now and her professional scruples.

Why not show Gina that them enjoying themselves together didn't have to screw up their professional relationship—because in the end, however distracting, however combustible they were together, it would only be sex. And that there really wasn't any blame to be apportioned for what had happened ten years ago any more—because as he had eventually discovered when he'd come to accept his true nature, it had been inevitable.

He took the exit off I-16 and headed into the city, towards the Historic District and home.

'With that in mind,' Gina piped up — the proprietary tone telling him she thought his silence had signalled acquiescence to her plans, 'I should probably check into a hotel during my stay.'

I don't think so, sugar.

He erased the itch of frustration and pasted on an easy smile. 'Now why would you do that?'

'Well, I…' she began, her tone not quite so sure.

'My home has a study with all the computer equipment you'll need to work on your plans for the mill while you're here,' he said, moving in his king to threaten her queen. 'And it'll save me having to drive to a hotel every time we want to work on them together. It's a whole lot more efficient if you stay at my place.'

'I'm still not sure…'

'Of course, if you're scared you won't be able to keep your hands to yourself?'

The prickle of irritation made it clear she hadn't spotted the trap. 'I'm perfectly capable of—'

'Then we don't have a problem, do we?' he cut in and rolled through the four-way stop sign that stood at the corner of Peachtree and Divine.

Checkmate, sugar.

Gina pushed the flicker of panic to the back of her mind at the knowledge that she'd just been rather neatly outmanoeuvred.

Don't be ridiculous.

They were both adults. He hadn't objected to her stipulation about no sex. In fact, he'd been remarkably unconcerned and accommodating—to the point of being a little ego-deflating, really. Seemed she might have overestimated her charms—and his intentions.

The car glided into a tree-lined square with a decorative stone fountain as its centrepiece.

'This is pretty. Where are we?' she asked, determined to soak up Savannah's elegant architecture and stop obsessing about the distracting man next to her.

'We're in the Southern Historic District and this is Divine Square. My place is on the far side.' He pointed past the fountain.

'It's beautiful.'

The imposing three-and four-storey Victorian houses stood back from the road on all four sides of the square behind high fences or fancy iron railings, their ornate balconies and colourful gingerbread trim vaguely reminiscent of New Orleans' French Quarter. But with the houses' imposing wooden shutters closed tight against the muggy heat and the peaceful patch of flower beds and scrubs surrounding the fountain devoid of tourists, the historic square projected a well-bred gentility in direct counterpoint to the loud, louche ambience of the Big Easy.

'Here we go.' He stopped in front of a Civil War-era mansion that took up one whole side of the square. He leaned across to pull a small black device out of the glove compartment, giving her an enticing whiff of sweat and soap, before he pressed the button and the gates swished open.

'How long have you lived here?' she asked, oddly depressed at the thought he might have shared this home with his ex-wife.

'My family have owned the house for generations. I moved in a few years back,' he replied, inadvertently answering her question and making the knot in her stomach release a little. 'After my mother passed it was either move back in, sell it or watch the place fall into disrepair. Option one seemed the easiest for now.'

After parking in the house's driveway, he clicked the button to close the gates, slung the device back in the glove box and switched off the ignition. He swivelled round in his seat, a wry smile curving those firm sensual lips. 'The place has eight bedrooms, but I can get my housekeeper to open up the pool house, if you'd prefer more privacy.'

'Right,' she said, biting down on her bottom lip and the idiotic urge to pout at just how accommodating he was being to her no-sex suggestion. 'That would be ideal.'

Her breathing accelerated as he climbed out of the car and skirted the bonnet to open the passenger door. Standing back, he swept his hand out to encompass a front garden planted with flowering scrubs and a giant weeping willow that cast the stairs leading up to the mansion's front entrance in glorious shade. 'Welcome to the Price family's humble home, Gina.'

There was nothing humble about it or the wickedly tempting gleam in those devastating blue eyes.

Accepting his offer of the pool house hadn't been cowardice—it had been insurance. Resisting him wouldn't be that hard.... If she set her mind to it.

But she drew her fingers out of his as he took her hand to help her out of the car—and mounted the steps alone.

CHAPTER TEN

IN THE DAYS that followed, Gina surprised herself—sticking religiously to her decision to keep her association with Carter professional while working out a killer media strategy for the mill.

That said, the only way to stick to her plan had been to keep Carter at arm's length. Luckily for her, he'd helped to facilitate her avoidance by providing her with a sporty little Mustang to use as a runaround. After mornings spent at the mill getting acquainted with Carter's staff and the factory's production processes, and studiously avoiding too much consultation time with the man himself, she could escape in the afternoon to do 'important research' in Savannah.

Which turned out to be a surprisingly fascinating endeavour. She'd never been to the South before, having always dismissed it based on popular stereotypes and one too many viewings of *Gone with the Wind*. But instead of discovering a city marred by the legacy of slavery and the civil war, Gina discovered a thriving metropolis founded on commerce that had since become a cultural melting pot. Speciality bookshops, retro ice-cream parlours, rehabbed movie theatres showing old classics and Internet cafés filled with students and tourists alike vied for space with the grand mansions and garden squares of the Historic District. Despite its stately grandeur Savannah was a vibrant hub of activity filled with the curious and the ambitious.

Carter himself seemed to fall comfortably between the two—his easy-going manner matched by a sharp intelligence and a killer business instinct. It was hard not to admire his single-mindedness—even when that single-mindedness was aimed squarely at her. Because while she had made the commitment to keep their relationship professional, she wasn't convinced Carter was entirely on board with it. Her suspicions were aroused her first morning at the pool house, when she'd woken up to the sound of rhythmic splashing coming from right outside the front door.

She'd flipped up the curtain while making her morning coffee to see who was using the pool and got an eyeful of bronzed male muscle soaking wet. An eyeful she had not been able to erase from her brain no matter how hard she'd tried.

On day three of her self-imposed exile, she heard the sound of Carter doing his morning laps in the pool and resisted the urge to flip the curtain up again. For about fifteen seconds.

She caught him as he levered himself out of the water and stood on the tiles drying himself—her throat dried to parchment as heat pounded into every one of her pulsepoints.

'Carter Price, you wicked tease,' she whispered on an exasperated hiss, her fingers trembling on the curtain.

Was it her imagination or were those skin-tight trunks doing even less to cover his package this morning?

She blew out a breath of frustration. No wonder the blasted man had offered her a chance to stay in the pool house. 'A more private place to stay, my butt. More like a ringside seat to temptation.'

His ridged six-pack tensed as he lifted his arms to dry his hair—making his abdomen resemble that of a Greek statue. Sunlight peeked through the willow trees that separated the pool enclosure from the rest of the mansion's walled garden and rippled over firm, tanned flesh. Gina's tongue darted out to lick dry lips as he looped the towel round his shoulders and glanced towards the pool house.

She dropped the curtain as if it had been electrified with a two-thousand-volt current.

Had he spotted her peeking?

She poured herself a cool glass of lemonade from the pitcher in the house's tiny fridge and ignored the weight sinking in her belly.

After three quick swallows, she marched into the house's small bathroom—to complete her own morning ritual.

Who cared if he had spotted her looking at his nearly naked body in those ludicrously revealing swimming trunks? Peeking didn't count.

As long as she didn't go out there and rugby tackle him to the ground—she was still sticking to her curfew. With no help from him.

The man was being deliberately provocative. And she hadn't risen to the bait. She'd been mature and sensible and disgustingly celibate for three whole days now, while living in his home and being subjected to his buff body less than three yards from her bedroom door every morning.

And managing not to make any reference to his exhibitionism during the hours they spent together gave her a free pass to sainthood.

That said, her abstinence had cost her. It had taken her several hours to fall into a fitful sleep each night, the evenings she spent with Carter at the big house only adding to her torment.

Because while she'd managed to keep the conversation entirely innuendo free, sticking to topics such as her work on the new website design, blogging strategies, the history of Savannah and even the American Civil War—which Carter referred to with a wry smile as 'The War of Northern Aggression'—

and she hadn't salivated once, or not in his presence anyway, the pressure had built each night anyway.

All those long lazy looks, all those wide easy smiles when she said something sharp or witty, all those considering hums of approval that rumbled up his chest when he listened with alarming intensity—were not remotely innocent. And the swimming, right outside her bedroom window.... That was the biggest tease of all.

But she was holding up.

She swallowed down the lump of lust and risked another peek. An odd mixture of regret and relief swooped into her stomach at the sight of the empty pool patio, the wet footprints on the sun-soaked tiles leading out of the walled garden back towards the house. The still surface of the water glinted, a visible echo of the shimmer of sensation rising up her spine.

While her behaviour so far had been exemplary, she had over a week to go. And as each day passed—she could feel her resistance crumbling.

She let the curtain drop, stripped off the T-shirt she wore to sleep in and stepped into the shower. Ten days wasn't that long. She'd gone nearly six months before that thoughtless night a week ago with Carter. She could handle ten days. Surely.

And then she'd be free and clear and have conclusive proof that she could do denial. When she had to.

But then she pressed the palm of her hand to the mound of her sex, felt the insistent throb of arousal as she pictured his torso—and that damn package defined to perfection behind black Lycra—and flicked on the cold tap. She shuddered as she stood under the frigid spray, and had to admit that cold showers were getting seriously old.

So old, in fact, that tonight she might have to confront Carter when he returned from the mill for their regular dinner date at the mansion and let him know she was wise to his little game—and she wasn't playing.

'So did you enjoy yourself in Savannah today?'

Gina placed her fork beside her plate with deliberate precision and eyed Carter, who was sitting across from her at the large walnut dining-room table with a typically assured smile on his face.

'Yes, thank you. I took some nice shots down by the river and along Decatur to illustrate the weblog I'm planning. But I don't think I need to stay any longer. I thought I'd catch a flight home tomorrow.' And if the thought made her feel a little down, it had no bearing on anything.

'I thought we agreed you'd stay a couple of weeks? You've only been here three days.'

'I thought we agreed to keeping this relationship professional,' she countered. 'But that was before I discovered you were an exhibitionist.'

The crinkle of a frown cleared from his brow to be followed by the knowing curve of his lips. 'So now it's my fault you can't multitask?'

She tapped a fingernail against the shiny walnut veneer and glared at him. 'I didn't say I couldn't multitask, I said I didn't want to—because it'll distract me.'

'No, actually, you said you weren't good at multitasking.' The curve widened into a grin. 'So what you need is more practice.'

'Your morning swim is unnecessarily provocative. And you know it,' she snapped, determined to refocus the argument where it belonged—with the blame for her frustration firmly on his shoulders.

'Provocative or proactive?' The wry tone thickened with innuendo. 'I'm real good at multitasking, sugar, and I'm ready and willing to show you how it's done.'

She narrowed her eyes, and wished she had Superman's ability to sear lead with a single glance. 'Has it ever occurred to you and your gigantic ego that maybe I don't want to sleep with you again?'

He leant back in his chair, the nonchalant grin widening. 'As me and my gigantic ego have caught you peeking more than once,' he drawled, 'we know you want to, so I'm figuring it's not me, or the sex, you're scared of, it's yourself.'

'Scared of…' She scoffed, or tried to as the dart of shame she'd suppressed for so long closed her throat. 'Don't be ridiculous. Why would I be scared of myself? Scared of what exactly?'

'You tell me,' he replied, the smile fading as his gaze sharpened—and she had the uncomfortable feeling he could see into her soul. 'You're the one who apologised for something that didn't have a damn thing to do with you. You're the one who called herself a tramp…. You're the one who's putting business before pleasure when there's no reason why we can't enjoy both while you're here. We're both consenting adults, we're both unattached at the moment, we both enjoy sex—especially with each other—and we're both too good at what we do to let something as inconsequential as sex distract us. So why shouldn't we go for it?'

She placed her napkin on the table, then stood, bracing her palms on the polished wood to disguise trembling fingers.

'Thank you for the commission. I'm going to do an amazing job. And thank you for your Southern hospitality.' She forced servility into her voice, searching for the professional distance. 'Savannah is a beautiful city, and I've enjoyed my stay here.' Give or take the odd sleepless night. 'But I think I'll pass on the free psychoanalysis *and* your generous offer of anonymous sex on the side. And head home tomorrow.' Where she should have stayed all along.

He stood as she left the room, the gallant gesture in contrast to the open hunger in his gaze as it met hers. She made herself take brisk, sure, sensible steps, despite the pulse of longing making her limbs lethargic.

He didn't know her, and he didn't know what she'd been through ten years ago. And he never would, because telling him now would be painful and pointless—and far too personal. But she had to admit that he'd been right about one thing. Her desire to avoid more intimacy between them had nothing whatsoever to do with the commission or her multitasking skills and everything to do with the man.

Because she'd discovered a long time ago that sex with Carter Price was never inconsequential.

Carter whispered an expletive as the door clicked closed, and threw down the napkin clutched in his fist.

Cute, Price. Real cute.

After three days of keeping his cool, of keeping his distance, of letting her have the time she needed to get over her misguided professional ethics, and being real careful not to show his frustration—and parading around on that damn pool terrace every morning like a prize stud—he'd had his moment and he'd screwed it up. Because he'd pushed. And he never pushed...

Mercy, had he actually used the word inconsequential? No wonder she'd heard the word anonymous instead.

He might as well have hoisted her onto the table, flipped up her skirts and torn off her panties again for all the finesse he'd used.

He crossed to the drinks cabinet, pushed aside the imported single malt whiskey he usually favoured to clasp the bottle of his father's locally distilled liquor that lurked at the back. He downed a generous slug, then flinched as it shot down his throat like a burning bullet and exploded in his stomach.

He thumped a fist to his chest, to restart his heart, and let out a harsh cough.

Gina Carrington might be the most sexually liberated woman he'd ever met, but she was still a woman. Which meant she deserved to be wooed, not bullied, into his bed.

Carter, honey, have you ever thought your desires might be a little unnatural? Delfina tells me her Jim doesn't expect her to do her marital duty more than once a month and yet you are pestering me every other night.

The long-forgotten memory of his young wife's barbed enquiry pierced through his frustration—bringing with it the crushing echo of guilt and humiliation. He shoved the bottle back into the cabinet, raked not-quite-steady fingers through his hair.

Where the hell had that come from? He wasn't that green kid any more, trying and failing to satisfy a woman whose needs had never matched his own. Women enjoyed his company now, in bed as well as out of it. And his marriage to Missy hadn't failed ultimately because of their sexual problems, but for a whole host of other reasons.

When he was sixteen and they'd first started dating, Missy Wainwright's sweet, peaceful, non-confrontational company had been his sanctuary from a home where his father's bullying, overbearing presence and his mother's rigid insistence that keeping up appearances was all that mattered had made him feel sullen and tense and disillusioned.

But after his father's death, and that incendiary one-night encounter with Gina Carrington—a woman who couldn't be sweet and peaceful even if you gagged her—he'd begun to see that Missy's sweetness stemmed from a lack of intelligent conversation, and her refusal to argue about anything openly was actually more passive-aggressive than peaceful and non-confrontational.

Missy had said she'd forgiven him, when he'd returned to

Savannah and confessed the sin he'd committed with Gina. But the knowledge had been there festering between them, the wounded expression she wore every time they had a disagreement reminding him without words that he was the one in the wrong—he was the one who couldn't be trusted. And the fact that he'd never been able to forget Gina—and how much he'd enjoyed sinning with her—only increased his guilt.

During the increasingly bitter, barren years of his marriage, he'd got a little fixated on the exquisite pleasure of that one night. The surge of excitement, of exhilaration when Gina kissed him and caressed him with such fervour in places Missy had barely been willing to touch—and made love to him with a fierce, untamed determination that told him she wanted him, that she accepted him despite his faults.

Missy's deflating words, the wounded look she'd wielded so effectively, faded as two searingly erotic visions of Gina took their place and merged into one. Not quite two weeks ago riding him to climax—and a decade before that as she impaled herself on his thrusting erection for the first time: her unguarded expression full of the same wild hunger he'd glimpsed from behind the pool house curtain that morning.

His heart kicked so hard he could hear it above the ticks of his mother's antique carriage clock on the mantel. The heavy weight of his erection strained for release against the confinement of his suit pants.

Maybe it was time he stopped kidding himself that his desire to have Gina again had nothing whatsoever to do with that night a decade ago. Was that why he'd screwed up this seduction so royally? Because a part of him was still desperate to prove his desires weren't unnatural and they never had been? Because he needed to recapture that addictive feeling of euphoria, that heady feeling of connection they'd shared under a maple tree in the campus grounds and on her nar-

row bed in Reese's house—and just under two week ago in
the cool lines of a New York hotel room.

Gina Carrington still had some weird hold over him. Or
rather, she had some weird hold over his body. Probably because she'd been his first. A hold he intended to break over
the next ten days. So he could sever for ever his ties to that
green, needy boy.

But to do that he had to get Gina to play ball.

So instead of standing here, drinking his old man's boot-
leg liquor and beating himself up about her decision to leave,
what he needed to do was get her to stay.

Yeah, Gina was a woman but she wasn't like any other
woman he'd ever met.

You couldn't reason with Gina, or cajole her, or control
her.... The only way to get what you wanted was to take it,
and give her what she wanted in return.

He walked to the door of the dining room, headed down
the corridor to the back of the house, purpose in every stride.

To hell with sense and caution and business scruples.

Raindrops splattered his face as he strode through the darkened gardens towards the pool house. The ominous grum-
ble of distant thunder had a grim smile lifting his lips—and
seemed mighty fortuitous in the circumstances.

Given that he was about to fight fire with fire... A mon-
soon might come in handy to ensure they didn't both get
burned.

Then he walked silently through the gate that led to the
pool patio and his erection hit critical mass. A dark figure
stood at the far end of the pool beneath the overhanging
branches of the willow tree. Her arms stretched skyward,
beckoning the rain forth to drench the thin silk of her blouse
and reveal the lacy bra beneath.

Seemed he wasn't the only one who needed relief from
the heat.

She twirled under the deluge, the sinuous movement effortlessly sensuous, artlessly sexy—and demonstrating the extent of the need she'd tried so hard to hide.

She was magnificent—and for the next ten days, he was going to make sure she was all his.

He stepped forward as the heavens opened and the rain soaked through his shirt and trousers in seconds. The ripple of lightning glimmered off the water and lit her face as her gaze darted to his.

She dropped her arms. Shock and desire made a devastating combination on her face as she stood completely still, observing him, then swept the damp hair over her shoulders—the bold, provocative move part instinct, part invitation but mostly challenge. The dark outline of her nipples jutted through her transparent clothing as the rain continued to pound down.

'I told you we're not going to do this,' she shouted above the clap of thunder. 'I'm leaving tomorrow.'

He could see her staggered breathing, but she didn't retreat when he reached her, or shrink away when he gathered a fistful of her wet hair, and drew her head back. Water slicked down her face and made her eyelashes glitter above the defiant glare.

'You're not going anywhere,' he yelled back. 'We need to finish this once and for all.'

She shuddered and braced her palms against his chest, but instead of pushing him away her fingers gripped, her gaze full of the sexual knowledge that had always inflamed his senses. 'And how exactly do you propose we do that?'

He wrapped his arm round her waist, yanked her towards him, grinding the painful erection against the soft, yielding flesh of her belly. 'The only way we know how.'

Then he slanted his mouth across hers—and plundered.

CHAPTER ELEVEN

WE NEED TO finish this once and for all.

Carter's ultimatum echoed through Gina's mind as she plunged her fingers into his hair, and their tongues tangled.

This wasn't the fun, teasing, flirtatious exploration of their New York encounter. This was raw, basic, elemental need. She had thought she could resist him. She'd been wrong.

As her fingers clutched the short curls at his nape and the rain pummelled them both, the fire consumed her. Sense and reason deserted her. Why couldn't they do this? He was right. They were consenting adults, they both enjoyed sex, especially with each other, and no one need ever know.

And how was she ever going to be able to rely on her new leaf with this burning hunger for him lurking in the background?

Wide palms gripped her hips and ground her against the thick ridge in his trousers. He lifted his head, water dripping off his brows, and shouted above the rain. 'Let's take this inside before we drown.'

Grasping her hand, he jogged to the pool house and dragged her inside. Wet clothes stuck to hot, damp skin as they battled together to get naked as fast as possible.

He tore her blouse, she ripped his shirt, but after a furious battle they touched flesh. She shivered as he hauled her close and they feasted on each other. Her back bumped against the closed door as he lifted her, positioning her to take him. Then he reared back and swore softly, letting her go.

'Damn it!' He grappled for his discarded trousers, retrieved the foil package, and sheathed himself.

'Good thinking, Batman.' She kissed him, framing his face with shaking hands. 'Now hurry up.'

'Yes, ma'am.' He boosted her into his arms, thumping her back against the door, and took her in one solid thrust.

The shocking fullness turned to exquisite pain, mind-blowing pleasure. He withdrew, thrust back—the movements harsh, rough, and lacking his usual finesse, but so perfect, so right. Tears stung her eyes as she rode the glorious wave to completion.

He shuddered and with an incomprehensible grunt followed her over seconds later.

They stood together, his fingers digging into her thighs, her legs hooked around his waist, his erection still huge inside her. The patter of slowing rain hitting the door masked the jagged pants of their breathing. He dropped his forehead to hers, and whispered, 'I think I just died and went to heaven.' She tightened her arms around his neck as he buried his face in her wet hair, the sudden urge to stay for ever in the semi-consciousness of afterglow overwhelming. She didn't want to worry about consequences. About right, or wrong. Sense or insanity. She just wanted to feel him inside her.

Easing out of her, he let her down gently. A single tear slipped over her lid—the moment of connection, of acceptance, gone. She shook off the sentimental thought and scrubbed away the tear with an impatient fist.

Don't get mushy, you ninny. This is sex. Great sex. You don't want more.

Holding his head, she lifted his face, and grinned.

'Isn't that sacrilegious?'

'What?' he asked, clearly a little dazed.

'Mentioning heaven after what we just did?'

'The hell you say.'

He grinned back at her. 'Which is exactly why you love me.'

She forced a smile, the casual use of the *L* word a shock. And not a pleasant one. 'That would be your ego talking,' she replied dryly.

She stepped out of his arms—needing distance. But a muscled arm banded round her waist, halting her retreat. 'Hey, we're not through here.'

He nuzzled her neck and sensation raced down her spine, the thick ridge of renewed arousal nestling between her buttocks.

'My ego wants to try out the bed.'

'Oh, it does, does it?' She turned, and draped her arms over his shoulders, locking her knees against the foolish fragility— then glanced down, pointedly. 'I must say, your ego has remarkable powers of recuperation.'

He tucked a finger under her chin, and raised her face. 'Only where you're concerned.'

'Good to know.' She forced flippancy into her voice. *Just great sex. Remember.*

Taking her hand, he crossed to the bed and in one smooth move swung her into his arms and then dumped her into the centre of the mattress. Laughter bubbled in her chest, forcing out the vulnerability. This could never be more for her, or for him, than a quick fling. So why stress about it? She didn't do ties, or commitments, because she hated regrets. And she had far too many of them already. Especially where Carter Price was concerned.

Lying down next to her, he combed his fingers through her hair and traced his thumb across her cheekbone. 'Damn, Gina, but you're irresistible.'

Her heart squeezed at the gleam of admiration in those

pure blue eyes. She held his wrist and lifted his hand away from her face. 'So are you. Which would probably explain why, despite my best intentions, this keeps happening.'

He toyed with a damp curl that hung over her shoulder, tantalisingly close to her breast, a slow smile forming. 'I'm hoping that means this isn't another one-off.' He lifted the curl to his lips and kissed it, the tenderness of the gesture causing the blood to thunder in her ears. 'And you're not still planning to run out on me tomorrow.'

'I think we both just proved neither of us are *that* good at denial.'

He dropped the curl, the smile widening. 'So is this a *thing*, or a *fling*?'

The mocking question eased the squeeze on her heart. 'A fling. But that's all it is. My flight back's in just over a week's time and that's when this will have to end.'

The broad smile didn't falter. 'Works for me.' His hand skimmed down her neck and cupped her breast, his thumb circling the rigid nipple. 'But no more dumb stuff about work.' His eyes met hers, the expression more determined than playful. 'What we do in bed together—and anywhere else we choose—hasn't got a damn thing to do with your commission. You got that?'

She stretched, trying to focus on the conversation while his absent caress sent sensation into her sex. 'Yes, boss.'

His eyebrows shot up and she laughed. Grabbing her wrists, he yanked her arms above her head and held her captive for a quick hard kiss. 'Damn, but I want you again, you little tease.'

'What's stopping you, Rhett?' She rubbed her leg against his, enjoying the feel of the soft hairs, the muscled flanks and the sight of his eyes dilating to black.

'Lord, give me strength,' he murmured, trapping her legs with one hard thigh. 'We're gonna have to take a rain check.'

He glanced out of the window at the dying storm. 'Literally. I
need more condoms. A lot more.' His gaze roamed over her.
'I'm thinking a whole box wouldn't go amiss.'

'Not a problem, sugar. Like all smart, responsible, twenty-
first-century women, I keep an emergency supply in my toiletry bag.' She reared up to kiss him on the nose, feeling
ridiculously perky, and carefree and relieved. There was no
need to read more into this fling than there actually was—
they had a history, but one he need never know about, and one
she had come to terms with a long time ago. 'I'll go get them.'

'Nuh-uh.' He snagged her round the waist as she launched
off the bed. 'Right now I'm a big fan of female emancipation,
but I'm still the guy. I'll get them.'

She laughed, the command delivered in a wry monotone
that was both stupidly macho and surprisingly cute. 'My
hero,' she purred, the endorphins shooting round her body
overriding the last of her caution. She lounged against the pillows and watched him march into the bathroom, gloriously
naked. A man on a mission.

She admired the tight buns as his bare butt disappeared
from view and sent up her own silent prayer of thanks. They
had just over a week to finally finish this. To satisfy the sexual hunger that had always burned so brightly, so insistently
between them. And this time there could be no harm done—
because she wasn't that wild, reckless, vulnerable girl any
more, but a smart, sorted career woman who…

'What the *Sam Hell*…?'

The startled oath had her shooting upright—the smug contentment faltering as she recalled exactly what else she kept
in her toiletry bag.

Carter emerged from the bathroom with a fistful of condoms in one hand, and the long column of moulded plastic
held delicately between the thumb and forefinger of his other
hand—as if it were an unexploded bomb. He cleared his throat

dramatically and held it up for inspection. 'Well, now. What do you have here, Miss Gina?'

She flopped back on the pillows, and stared at the ceiling fan, struggling to quell the blush blossoming across her chest. 'You found Justin.'

'You gave it a *name*?' The question came out on a choke of outrage.

She inched up on her elbows, the blush subsiding as her lips quirked. 'Well, of course I did. I don't want to be getting it on with a stranger.' What was there to be embarrassed about? If a smart, responsible, twenty-first-century woman was single and intended to stay that way, a vibrator was essential equipment.

He made a sound in his throat as if he were choking. 'I think I just died and went to hell! What did you call it, again?'

She covered her mouth to suppress the unladylike snort of amusement. 'Justin.'

'Hell, I thought so.' He peered at it. 'Not only did you give it a name, you gave it a sissy name.'

The snort popped out, tinged with mock outrage. 'Justin is not a sissy name. I happened to have a major crush on Justin Timberlake once upon a time. So it seemed appropriate.'

'Sugar, I don't know what kind of guys you've been dating. But nothing about this *tool* is appropriate. It isn't even anatomically correct. No guy's got that much heft this side of an elephant.'

She giggled, crawling across the bed to perch on the edge and cup him. She stroked, and hummed deep in her throat, her gaze sweeping down to assess the firm flesh as it swelled and hardened. Her gaze swept back up to peer at him through lashes that fluttered demurely. 'I don't know... You seem to be giving Justin a fairly good run for his money.'

'Right, that does it.' Flipping the vibrator over his shoulder, he gave her shoulders a shove, tumbling her onto the bed. He climbed on top, caging her in, his rough chuckles mingling with her giggles.

'Hey, be careful with Justin!' she said, still channelling the mock outrage. 'He wasn't exactly cheap.'

'Sweetheart, in case you haven't figured this out yet...' He rubbed the heel of his palm against her mound, the dire warning in his voice promising all sorts of delicious retribution '...from here on in, you are dumping *Justeen* in favour of a real man.'

She laughed out loud, sucking in a breath when he licked one thrusting nipple and drew it into his mouth. The areola tightened and throbbed. 'Yes, but do you have seven different settings?' she demanded on a breathless sigh.

He blew softly on her aching nipple, lifting his head when she groaned. The confidence in his gaze was as arousing as the expert stroke of his fingertips on the slick wet flesh between her thighs. 'Sugar, when you're as good as I am, you only need the one.'

She was still laughing as he stroked her over the edge.

CHAPTER TWELVE

IN THE BLISSFUL days that followed, Gina worked hard to create a magnificent new website and excellent media strategy for the Price Paper Consortium. She worked even harder at fulfilling every prurient sexual fantasy she had ever had about the consortium's CEO. And harder still at ensuring her emotions didn't get in the way of the good time she was having, and the even better sex.

But as the days passed a hitch appeared in her plan that involved an unfortunate discovery. Carter Price was as irresistible out of bed as he was in it.

And if she didn't know better, she could have sworn he had orchestrated that giddy glide into romance, almost as carefully as he had orchestrated their red-hot ride into lust.

Why else would he have organised an evening watching classic Hollywood movies at the retro cinema a ten-minute walk from his home—and then made her heart flip-flop by necking with her in the back row? Why else would he have insisted on holding her hand during their lazy afternoon stroll through the redevelopment of trinket shops and parkland on River Street? Or whispered wicked suggestions in her ear to make her laugh as they browsed the antiquarian delights in a dusty basement bookshop?

Even at the mill, where she insisted on them maintaining a respectable distance in front of his employees, his sharp, insightful and always enthusiastic comments about her ideas had become as seductive as all those casually possessive gestures and throwaway displays of affection. She felt as if she'd been caught in the silken web of his friendship—become a prisoner to all that charm and charisma and affability, powerless to resist the steely determination that lurked beneath.

Dating Carter Price was certainly unlike any of her other dating experiences—which, although not nearly as prolific as most people believed, fell into two distinct categories: the standard 'hot, short and sweet', or, on those rare occasions when she didn't end the affair soon enough, 'hot, short and not-so-sweet'. Carter should have fallen easily into the first category. That had been the plan. But he wasn't hot, he was scorching, and as the day approached when she would have to leave Savannah and return to her single life 'short and sweet' was becoming 'short and potentially sticky'. Sticky in a way that confused and disturbed her, because the single life she loved was starting to seem boring and even a little lonely simply because it wouldn't have Carter in it.

Gina stretched limbs pleasantly sore from the night-time's activities and rolled onto her side to contemplate the man lying next to her in the generous tester bed—and all the reasons why their fling was starting to bother her.

She frowned. And that was another thing. They'd relocated to his palatial bedroom in the main house after their first night at the pool house, Carter insisting that the queen bed was way too cramped for them to explore each other properly. Given the scope of exploration he'd had in mind—which even she, with her suitably filthy mind, hadn't anticipated—she had to concede he'd had a point. And staying in his room, with its solid, intricately carved mahogany furniture and the wide French doors that opened onto a charming balcony overlooking the square, hadn't exactly been a chore.

But as the morning sun streamed in, illuminating the hand-

some face that had captivated her a decade ago, she also had
to concede that moving into the main house was just another
in a long line of concessions she'd agreed to without putting
up much of a fight. Right from the moment he'd looked at
her across the bar in The Standard Hotel with that dangerous allure in his eyes, she'd been giving in to him over and
over again—and that was bothering her too, almost as much
as her reluctance to walk away from him in a few days time.

She searched his face for clues as to how he'd managed
to slip under her guard—and make her crave his attention.
She studied the dark brows, that tempting dent in his chin
and the small creases of amusement at the edge of his mouth
that he wore even in sleep. She blew out an unsteady breath.
No wonder she was captivated—and behaving like a rabbit
caught in the headlights of an oncoming freight train. The
man was a total studmuffin, just as Reese had described
him—and that was without even factoring in the effect of
those killer blue eyes that could tempt a saint into fornica-
tion when he was awake.

He shifted in his sleep, mumbling something before a
heavy hand came to rest on her hip. An errant curl of dark
hair fell across his forehead. She smoothed it off again with
a fingernail and his eyelids snapped opened. She snatched
her hand back. Too late. She was already trapped in that penetrating blue gaze.

'Hey there,' he growled. His fingers tightened on her hip
and he eased her closer, the familiar morning cuddle something she'd got too accustomed to as well. 'How you feeling,
this bright and beautiful morning, Miss Gina?'

*Not as safe as I'd hoped. Why do you have to be so irre-
sistible, Carter Price?*

Swallowing down the solid object lodged in her throat,
she lifted the sheet to inspect the equally solid object nudg-
ing her belly. 'Not as perky as you, obviously.'

He yawned, and stretched through a rumble of self-satisfied laughter. 'Well now, sugar. That's just a natural male reaction to waking up beside a beautiful...' The suggestive comment drifted to a halt as he squinted into the sunlight, then jerked into a sitting position and thrust a hand through his hair. 'Damn it, what time is it?'

'About ten, at a conservative estimate.'

He swore, whipped back the sheet and jumped out of bed, protective hands cupping his morning erection as he raced to the dresser.

'What's the matter?' She sat up, hugging the sheet to her bosom, and smiled, his panicked antics dissolving the tightness in her throat.

Honestly, what on earth was she worrying about? She'd be leaving soon and, while it might be a bit more of a wrench than she'd anticipated, nothing would make her change that. Of course she felt drawn to him, in a way she hadn't with other men, because they had a past. But that didn't mean they had a future.

'It's the weekend today,' she supplied.

'It's Sunday,' he declared, as if that explained everything. He dug out a pair of boxers and hopped across the room while shoving a foot into them—nearly falling over en route to the wardrobe. The resultant muttered curse elicited a chuckle from her ringside seat on the bed.

'As much as I'm enjoying the show,' she said, the now familiar giggles floating out as he yanked a perfectly pressed white linen shirt out of the wardrobe, 'isn't it bad karma to be swearing like that on a Sunday?'

He swung round, buttoning the shirt. 'Very funny.' Strolling back to the bed, he tugged the sheet out of her hands, his eyes glittering with retribution.

'Hey,' she protested, only to have the sheet flipped off entirely.

'No need to look so smug, Miss Gina. Because you're coming with me.'

She scrambled to retrieve the sheet. 'Says who? And where exactly do you think you're taking me?'

'To church. Where else?' He wrestled the sheet away with ease when her fingers went numb.

'I haven't been inside a church since I was sixteen and I got kicked out of St Bude's.'

'Why did they kick you out?'

She sent him a glare while trying to grab back the sheet. 'I seduced the biology teacher,' she replied, hoping to shock him with the truth—and get her hands on the stupid sheet.

Instead of looking shocked, though, he only laughed, balling up the sheet and tossing it across the room. 'Lucky guy.'

The lack of censure in his gaze as it roamed appreciatively over her exposed flesh made her cheeks heat. She tossed her hair over her shoulders, refusing to acknowledge the glow of contentment. So what if her many youthful transgressions didn't appear to bother him in the slightest? It was only because he was as big a reprobate as she was, and consequently unshockable.

'Sounds to me like you're definitely overdue for a visit to church, though,' he murmured. 'You need to atone for that sin and a whole lot more I happen to have firsthand knowledge of.'

'Not a chance.' She surrendered the sheet in favour of a mad dash to the bathroom—only to have him capture her in mid-flight. Her breath whooshed out as he scooped her up and her back hit his chest.

'FYI, honey,' he whispered into her hair, 'you'll have to cut down your two-hour morning shower. The service starts at eleven. And we don't want to be late.'

She struggled in earnest. 'Don't be ridiculous. I'm not going. I'd probably get struck by lightning.'

'God's a whole lot more forgiving than you think.' He nipped her ear lobe, laughing when she shuddered. 'If I've never been struck by lightning, I figure you're safe from divine retribution too.' The soft, seductive murmur of his breath turned her knees to jelly. 'Although, you may want to avoid going into the Lord's house the way God intended you.' He toyed with a nipple.

She slapped his hand away and escaped from his embrace, aroused now and more than a little disturbed by the invitation—and his insistence. 'You are kidding, right?'

He had to be. Surely? She didn't want to go to church. It would make her feel uncomfortable and hypocritical. Bringing back far too many memories of Sunday morning services at a succession of different boarding schools when she'd listened to the sermons with half an ear and refused to repent her many sins. And she definitely didn't want to go to church with Carter. There would be people he knew there. People he might introduce her to. People who might still be in touch with Marnie. But, worse than that, those same people might assume they were a couple. And they weren't.

'No, I'm not kidding,' he said, with strained patience, landing a playful slap on her butt when she stood rooted to the spot. 'Now put a fire under it. I'd hate to drag you there naked, and scandalise the minister. But I will if I have to.'

She grabbed the discarded sheet from the floor and wrapped it around her body, protecting herself from that far-too-possessive gaze, but not managing to do much for the shiver of unease.

'Carter, I am *not* going to church with you.'

His eyebrows winged up. 'Why not?'

'Because...' She wound the sheet tighter. 'Because people you know will be there.'

His mouth tilted in a puzzled smile. 'Uh-huh, so?'

Good grief, he actually was serious.

'So? So?' Her voice rose as irritation got the better of her. 'Meeting them would be...' *Wrong.*

'Would be what?' he asked over his shoulder, while selecting a suit from the wardrobe and tugging the trousers off the hanger.

'Pointless. Unnecessary,' she ground out, groping for the appropriate word. 'Misleading.'

His brows flattened into a frown as he zipped his trousers. 'Why don't you let me decide that?' he replied as if he hadn't just lost his mind. He shrugged on the suit jacket, then lifted her dress off the chair beside the bed and lobbed it to her—the same lemon-yellow shift dress that he'd peeled off her the night before. 'Put that on—it'll work.'

She caught the dress, and clasped it to her chest—starting to feel overwhelmed by that cast-iron will again, and not liking it one bit. 'Carter, you're not listening to me. There is no way I'm going to church with you.'

He approached her, looking impossibly debonair in the dark grey single-breasted suit. Placing warm palms on her shoulders, he massaged the tight muscles, digging into the knots of tension and making awareness skitter across her collarbone. 'I want you there—why are you worried about people I know meeting you? I'm not.'

You should be, she wanted to say, but she didn't, because it would make her sound cowardly and insecure. And she was neither of those things. Or she hadn't been until she'd fallen under Carter Price's spell again.

She gulped, refusing to give in to the flutter of panic— or the shimmer of arousal. And stepped out of reach of his magic hands.

Don't overreact. He's just a guy. He can't cast a spell on you unless you let him.

'Don't be silly—I'm not worried.' She was petrified and

she wasn't even sure why, but he definitely didn't need to know that.

'I guarantee they'll all be real polite,' he said lazily, but his eyes narrowed, his gaze sharpening. 'Southern manners mean they'll have to be.' He brushed a thumb across her cheek and sent her an easy smile. The panicked flutter intensified, as if she had a hummingbird trapped in her oesophagus. 'And anyhow, you don't have a choice.' His voice lowered in warning. 'Either you come peaceably or I'm going to cart you there over my shoulder.'

The teasing smile was still in place, but she could see the determined tilt of his chin and the muscle in his jaw flexing—and she couldn't be sure he was joking. Ordinarily she would have relished the fight, but right now her knees were too watery and the pulse of awareness in her belly too insistent to guarantee a win. So she went for the only option she had left—until she could think of another—grudging surrender. 'Fine, great, I'll go! But don't expect me to enjoy it.'

The teasing smile widened into a triumphant grin. 'This is the Riverside Christian Congregational Church, sugar. Attendance is about saving your immortal soul and making good business connections. And if you're a pillar of the community like me, you're not allowed to skip it or people will talk. But enjoyment is entirely optional.'

'Fabulous.' She marched to the bathroom, planning to indulge in her usual lengthy morning shower just to spite him—and hopefully postpone the inevitable. But before she had a chance to slam the door, she heard the wry comment from behind her. 'Make it quick. You've got ten minutes before I come in to get you.'

Blast the man, how did he read her so easily?

Ten minutes later she found out he wasn't joking about that either.

CHAPTER THIRTEEN

'ARE YOU GOING to sulk the whole day or can I expect a smile some time soon?'

Carter grinned at the surly expression Gina flicked his way from the passenger seat. He knew it was a cliché, but she looked cute when she was mad, especially with the wind blowing that sunshine-yellow dress against her figure as they drove down the river road.

'You know, you still haven't told me why you're so keen to drag me to church today.' She scowled at him. 'Apart from the obvious reason, of course.'

He shifted gear to take the bend and chuckled. 'Which is?'

'That you seem to get off on making me mad.'

She'd got that right, so he decided not to deny it. 'Hey? Is it my fault you look so damn sexy when you pout?'

She rolled her eyes. 'I'm going to be doing a lot more than pouting if this ordeal turns out as badly as I expect.'

He reached over the console to place a reassuring hand on her thigh—touched by the quiver of uncertainty in her voice.

He had to admit at first it had been a game getting her to hold his hand in public, getting her to cuddle up in bed each morning, hearing that sigh of surrender every time he increased the intimacy between them that bit more. But in the last week, he'd become addicted to pushing her boundaries, to seeing how far he could take it—and it didn't feel like a game any more. Because of that band that tightened around his heart now, every time the wary look flickered into her eyes when he got too close. For a woman who oozed sexual confidence, those moments of vulnerability intrigued and fascinated him and made him want to break down her barriers—to understand where her insecurities came from, and wipe them away.

He knew part of it had to do with her old man, whom she'd told him in a rare moment of candour had kicked her out as a teenager, but he couldn't quite shake the unpleasant thought that it also had something to do with him and what had happened between them a decade ago. Because every time he tried to talk about that, she shut up like a clam.

'Come on, sugar.' He patted her leg through the silk, the amusement gone. 'It won't be that bad, I swear.'

He caught her sceptical frown before returning his attention to the road.

'Why *do* you want me there?' she asked, again, putting him on the spot.

He didn't really have an answer, or certainly not one he wanted to admit to. How could he tell her that he wanted people to know they were together? That he'd gotten tired of the fiction that this was all just about sex? Without it seeming as if he was trying to back out of their deal?

He knew she'd be leaving soon and he was good with that. Ever since the failure of his marriage he'd made a point of not getting too attached to the women he dated.

But even if this wasn't permanent, he'd never liked subterfuge and he liked even less Gina's desire to keep their affair a secret. Why couldn't they enjoy each other's company in public as well as private? And while *he* knew that taking her to his family's church would make people think they were serious, she didn't know that, and he sure wasn't going to tell her. So what was she so damned scared of?

'No particular reason,' he lied smoothly. 'I just figured it would be cool to have you there, introduce you to some folks.' It was a non-answer and he could tell she knew it when he heard her scoff above the hot rush of wind.

'You know what drives me completely insane? The way you either answer a question with another question or give me an answer that means precisely nothing.'

He huffed out a chuckle. 'That's bull. I'm an open book.' He'd sure as hell been a lot more forthcoming about his past than she had. 'Go ahead and ask me anything you want.'

She swung round in the passenger seat and only then did it occur to him he might have given her too much rope. 'All right, then, answer me this: why did you despise your father?'

He mentally banged his head against the steering wheel. He hadn't seen that one coming. 'Why would you want to know that?'

'That doesn't happen to be another question you've just asked me, does it?'

Busted.

While he didn't much like getting caught on his own hook, he figured it would be smarter now not to give her the satisfaction of seeing him squirm.

Slowing the car to pull into the packed parking lot of the Riverside Church, he forced the words out on an indifferent monotone as he cruised into the only available slot at the end of the row. 'When I was fifteen, I caught my daddy making out with one of the help in my mama's parlour.'

'Making out? What exactly does that entail?'

He slung his arm over the wheel and stared at her, careful to keep his expression bland. 'He had his pants round his ankles, the girl was on her knees in front of him and his face looked like he was about to bust a blood vessel. Is that clear enough?'

He'd raised his voice, the old anger giving him away, but

instead of looking shocked or disgusted her eyes went dark with sympathy. 'Nasty,' she said. 'What did you do?'

'I told my mother and she went nuts.' He relaxed into the seat, the old anger dissolving in a pool of resignation. 'Not because of his *indiscretions*—she already knew about them—but because I'd had the bad manners to mention them.' He turned to Gina, the memory leaving a bitter taste. 'I knew they weren't madly in love with each other—I'd never seen them so much as kiss each other in public or in private. But until then I had no idea the marriage was such a dishonest sham. I promised myself if I ever got married it would be different. I would never cheat or lie to myself or my wife.' Damn, what a self-righteous hypocrite he'd been. 'Ironic, huh?'

Gina's pulse throbbed painfully in her neck. She hadn't expected his honesty and she didn't know how to make amends for the disillusionment that shadowed his eyes. 'I'm so sorry I made you break your promise.'

He shook his head and laughed, the deep rumble both genuinely amused and oddly comforting. 'Gina, sugar, no, you didn't.' He cupped her cheek. 'Meeting you eventually made me see I'd been kidding myself. My only regret now is that I didn't figure that out before I got into a marriage that was an even bigger lie than my parents'.'

She pulled his hand away from her face, knowing she couldn't have this conversation while he was touching her with such affection. But it was the first insight he'd given her into his marriage, and she couldn't stop herself from asking: 'How was it a lie?'

His gaze left hers and for a moment she felt sure he wouldn't answer, but then he shrugged. 'In a lot of ways.'

'What ways?'

The rueful grin returned. 'I believe you told me that night

that marrying a woman I had no knowledge of in the bedroom might end badly. Turns out you were right.'

'The *sex* was a problem?' Gina gasped, astonished, and unable to deny the sweet rush of vindication.

'Let's just say, she wasn't as enthusiastic about it as I was. Or you are.'

'That's not good,' she replied, stupidly pleased that the Virgin Queen of her imagination had been a little frigid after all.

'No, it sure isn't. It wasn't our biggest problem, but it felt big enough. Especially as I'd found out how good it could be...' He paused to clear his throat. 'With you.'

She should have stopped there, and let it go, this was all water way under the bridge now, but the sweet rush had turned to a torrent—and seeing the approval in his eyes only made it more intoxicating. 'What other problems did you have?'

'Eventually? Way too many to count.' The flush of colour hit his cheeks and the rush of vindication turned to one of sympathy. 'Before we were married she'd made me feel special,' he continued. 'She never challenged me, never contradicted me, never tried to tell me what to do like my daddy did. But then he died and I spent the night with you—and what we had didn't seem so special any more.' He gave his head a solemn shake. 'She said she'd forgiven me, that she still loved me, but she didn't trust me...' He sent her a wry look. 'And how could I blame her?' He shrugged. 'Whenever we argued, she always let me know I'd been the one to screw up our marriage before it had even started. Eventually, I began to wonder if I'd ever loved her—which only made me feel more guilty.'

Gina felt her throat close—choking on the knowledge he'd imparted so casually. 'You didn't love Missy?' she whispered, the shock twisting her stomach into knots.

He shook his head and her lungs seized—the sharp pain an echo of the agony she'd spent so long denying.

He banged his thumb against the steering wheel, his voice
a tense monotone as he continued. 'Finally I stopped being
such a gutless coward and asked for a divorce. Things got
even uglier for a while. Marnie stopped talking to me and
left Savannah for good.' He blew out a breath. 'But at least I
finally figured out I sucked at being a husband.'

Gina stared at him, the brittle sunlight making her eyes
water, and the knowledge that he'd suffered so much too making her heart hurt. 'I don't think that necessarily follows.'

'I don't see how you could draw any other conclusion,' he
murmured, his head bent.

'Did you cheat on Missy while you were married?'

His head jerked up. He looked startled and annoyed at the
accusation. 'Hell, no.'

'Then—while I know I'm hardly a disinterested party—I'd
say you're being overly generous to your ex-wife.'

'How do you figure that?'

'If she couldn't trust you, why on earth did she agree to
marry you?' she said, the knowledge that Missy had never
understood him, and never appreciated him, making the pain
lance through her. Why had she given up so easily? Let him
go without a fight? 'And frankly, holding that one night over
you like the Sword of Damocles for the rest of your marriage
sounds pretty manipulative to me.' And not much like the actions of a woman in love. 'It takes two to make a marriage
work and it doesn't sound as if she was doing her fair share.'

The chime of the church bell broke the pregnant silence
in the car.

He raked his fingers through his hair, sweat slicking his
brow. 'We better get in there before we melt.'

'Yes,' she said, grateful for the interruption—and the
chance to get her emotions back under control.

'Thanks,' he said, helping her out of the car, and her heart
leapt into her throat. 'You're right, Missy was pretty manip-

ulative, and I guess I was so busy blaming myself, I never saw that before.'

He squeezed her hand as they walked towards the redbrick church building—which looked drab and utilitarian, unlike the brightly dressed congregation hurrying to get inside. As they slipped into the air-conditioned darkness and took seats in the back pew she tugged her hand out of his. But panic continued to claw at her throat and the sweat became clammy as it dried on her skin.

What the hell was she doing here? Letting herself revisit feelings that had nearly destroyed her once and she now knew had the potential to destroy her all over again? She'd assumed those wayward emotions couldn't trip her up a second time. That after what she'd endured and survived as a teenager, she was far too mature, far too resilient and self-reliant to make the same mistake again.

But the bubble of hope that had lodged under her breastbone told a very different story.

She needed to get away from him, get away from here, before she risked regressing into that wild, needy, insecure girl who had fallen hopelessly in love with Carter Price one warm summer night—and lived to regret it.

Way to go, Price. What made you shoot your mouth off like that?

It rattled him that he'd told Gina stuff he'd never told another soul. But what had rattled him a whole lot more was her response, and how it had finally lifted the weight he'd carried for so long over the failure of his marriage.

Luckily the pastor had been filled with the holy spirit this morning and the sermon had lasted nearly an hour, giving him time to settle. But as he bowed his head, reciting the Lord's Prayer from memory, he saw Gina fidgeting with the hymnal. He laid a hand over hers, but she stiffened and drew them away.

Frustration gripped. Why was she so tense and skittish?

After the service, he ushered her into the Fellowship Hall for the superb beverages and snacks the church ladies provided and the polite conversation that always followed—ignoring the glare that said clearer than words, 'I'd like to leave now.'

While the urge to show her off had been replaced during the never-ending sermon by the burning desire to take her back to his bed and show her a different kind of heaven, he wasn't going to indulge it.

She meant more to him than just a roll in the hay—and he was sick of pretending that great sex and her commission were all that existed between them. He'd told her about his marriage, and it meant a lot to know she didn't judge him, the way he'd always judged himself.

He didn't want her to go hightailing it back to New York. He wanted her to stay in Savannah, to see where this might lead. While he wasn't laying any bets on the long haul, one thing he'd learned from his hell of a marriage was that you had to be honest about your feelings—and, damn it, he had feelings for Gina. And he knew she had feelings for him too.

Why she refused to admit them, he had no idea, but he intended to find out. Because he was dammed if he was going to let her shut him out any longer.

CHAPTER FOURTEEN

'I NEED ANOTHER SHOWER.' Gina flung her purse on the bed and yanked the pins out of her hair. Agitation crawled over her skin to add to the clammy layer of sweat. Agitation and something that felt unpleasantly like fear.

They'd hardly spoken on the drive back but she'd sensed his frustration—his usually fluid, graceful movements jerky and tense as he drove home—and she knew his mood wasn't much better than hers. So she made a Herculean effort to keep a lid on her own temper.

She needed to leave, this afternoon. And she wanted to do it quickly and quietly and as painlessly as possible—which meant for once in her life she needed to avoid making a scene.

Kicking off her shoes, she headed towards the bathroom, but a hard hand gripped her upper arm and swung her round to face him.

'Don't you think it's about time you stopped sulking?' The surly, condescending tone was too much—even for Hercules. 'Everyone was real polite, just like I said they would be. And they liked you, just like I knew they would. So I don't know what's got you so riled up.'

She wrestled her arm free. 'Sulking? You think this is sulking? I'm not sulking, I'm so mad at you I could smack you, so I'd strongly advise you keep your hands off me.'

His eyes flared, a dark, dangerous, electric blue, and instead of taking the warning he grasped both her arms and dragged her to him until they were nose to nose. 'You want to smack me? Honey, I've been resisting the urge to put you over my knee since we walked into the house. So don't tempt me!'

The last thread on her control snapped and then detonated like a firecracker. She struggled against his grip as the fear and panic that had been building all week—every time he touched her as if he cared, every time he held her with too much tenderness, every time he looked at her as if she mattered to him—and had exploded earlier when he'd told her about his marriage, lashed out and took control of her tongue.

'How dare you pretend that I'm the one in the wrong here? You made me participate in that farce when you knew I didn't want to. This isn't a relationship. It's a fling. That's what we agreed and now you're trying to move the goalposts without my consent. I'm not your girlfriend, and I don't want to be.'

And if she could just make herself believe that, everything would be okay again.

'And I certainly didn't sign up for that grilling I got from the ladies at your church who obviously now think we're madly in love and you're about to declare your intentions.' She could feel her anger gaining force and velocity at the memory of the subtly probing interrogation she'd had to endure over iced tea and butter-pecan cookies. 'So I think it's probably best that we call it quits and I leave now.'

His fingers went slack, the stricken look shocking her into silence and making her realise how much she'd said. She brushed away the stupid tear that trickled down her cheek, hating herself for giving so much away.

'Damn, Gina. Where the hell did that come from?'

Inadequacy and panic writhed in her stomach like venomous snakes—she couldn't let him see, she couldn't let him know how easily he could hurt her.

'Nowhere.' She drew in an unsteady breath, and struggled

to regain her composure. If he saw a weakness he'd exploit it—and get even further under her guard. 'I'm fine. I simply feel this *fling* has reached its natural conclusion. And I'd like to leave.'

'Stop lying to me and to yourself,' he said, the dogged determination in his tone making the fear increase. 'This stopped being a fling days ago—for both of us. I'm not even sure it was *ever* just about the sex. Even ten years back, at Hillbrook. And you know it too, or you never would have come to The Standard to give me that dumb apology. What I wanna know is why you're too damn scared to admit it.'

She stiffened her spine, but couldn't look him in the eye. 'There is no why. I'm just not the sort of woman who makes those kinds of attachments. And I never have been.'

'Uh-huh.' He circled her arm, stroking the inside of her elbow with his thumb when a shiver ran through her. 'So how come you're shaking?'

She drew her arm out of his grasp, rubbed skin suddenly chilled despite the warm sunlight flooding through the window. 'Don't touch me,' she said, biting into her bottom lip to stop it trembling.

'Whatever it is, you can tell me.' He touched his fingers to her cheek but she jerked her head back.

'No, I can't. I don't want to.' But as soon as she'd said the words, she knew she'd given away too much.

'Is it because of your old man? Is it because he kicked you out when you were still a kid? I know how that goes—my daddy made me feel like dirt too. It makes it hard to trust people, to trust how you feel.'

'Don't psychoanalyse me.' Her whole body began to tremble but she forced herself to look him in the eye and keep the emotion, the need, on lockdown, the way she had learned to do with her father. The way she'd learned to do with him. 'You don't know anything about my relationship with my father.'

'Okay, then, why don't you tell me? Tell me why he kicked you out. What did you do that was so terrible?'

He was standing too close, looking at her in a way that threatened to crash through every last one of her defences. The panic and fear became so huge, the only way to save herself was to hit out. 'If you must know, I came back from college in the US pregnant with a married man's child.'

'*What?*' His face went blank with shock—but there was no doubting he'd made the connection, when he raked shaking fingers through his hair and murmured, 'Oh, hell, Gina, I'm sorry.'

The old misery, the cruel loneliness, the bitter agony of loss and rejection rose up her throat like bile. She swallowed, desperate to push it back down.

She couldn't bear his sympathy, or his guilt, not now, not ever, so she shut herself away in that place she'd found where she could always be safe, always remain invulnerable—and recited the details as if their baby had died inside someone else. 'My father insisted I get rid of it. I refused. So I ended up living in a bedsit in Bayswater, working nights in a pub—and discovering that being a grown-up is a lot harder than it looks.'

He cursed under his breath. 'Why didn't you contact me? Why didn't you let me know? I would have helped.'

'Why would I contact *you*?' She put all the bitterness she could into the question to maintain the charade—and bury the hurt deep. 'You went back to your fiancée. What was there to say? It was a one-night stand.' Even if she'd tried to delude herself it could have been so much more. 'And in the end I didn't need your help. Because, thankfully, I lost the baby.'

It wasn't a lie, not really, she *had* been thankful in the end—after all the tears and the soul-searching and the mind-numbing grief. Thankful that she would never get the chance to screw up motherhood, the way she'd managed to screw up everything else.

'I'd managed to pull my life together in the process and get clear of my father,' she added, when he didn't respond. 'So it was all good.'

'How could it be good?' The shock cleared from his eyes to be replaced by hurt and confusion—and temper. 'If I'd had any idea, I never would've gone through with the wedding. You should have told me. I had a right to know.'

'Maybe.'

'And why the hell didn't you tell me *now*? We've been sleeping together for over a week, living in each other's pockets, and you didn't think it was worth mentioning?'

'No, I didn't.'

'I don't get it,' he said, the anger edged with disbelief. 'How could I be so damn wrong about you? I thought we had something going here.'

'Well, you thought wrong.'

'I never would have guessed anyone could be so hot in the sack and yet so heartless out of it.'

She let the accusation wash over her, like all the others.

He can't hurt you, unless you let him.

'I suppose that's one of the many mysteries of the universe, isn't it, Lover Boy.' She scooped her purse up off the bed, slung it over her shoulder, and fisted her fingers on the strap so he wouldn't see them shaking. 'I'll catch a cab to the airport. If you could have my luggage sent on, I'd appreciate it. I'll email you when the website and blog are live.'

He didn't say anything as she walked away. But while the panic pushing against her chest began to ease as she ran through the mansion's hallways, the pain she'd spent ten years running away from turned into a living, breathing thing—as sharp and relentless as it had ever been as it consumed her.

CHAPTER FIFTEEN

'GINA, I NEED a favour.' Reese's furious whisper interrupted Gina's listless gaze out of the large mullioned window of the Manhattan city clerk's office.

'A favour, right.' She forced a smile, trying to get into the party spirit, which had eluded her ever since they'd arrived twenty minutes ago at the newly refurbished, and suitably ornate Manhattan Marriage Bureau in preparation for Cassie's wedding.

Reese threaded an arm through Gina's. 'Are you sure you're okay? You look exhausted?'

Gina sighed, wondering why on earth she'd bothered to spend half an hour plastering on foundation. 'I had the flu that's been going around,' she said, giving the stock excuse she'd prepared earlier, after a similar interrogation from both Marnie and Cassie when they'd all convened at Amber's Bridal two days ago, to bully Cassie into picking out a proper wedding gown. 'But I'm on the mend now.'

Or I will be, eventually.

What a fool she'd been, to think she could carry on an affair with Carter and not plummet back down the black hole that had claimed her once before. If she hadn't been feeling so fragile she'd have kicked her own backside.

Reese gave her arm a gentle squeeze. 'So that's why you disappeared off the radar and bailed on all the party planning.' She sent her a curious glance. 'You could have let me know. I happen to be a champion pamperer. My chicken soup is legendary.'

'Sorry, I didn't feel up to company,' Gina replied, deflecting the sympathy she knew she didn't deserve. Lying to her friends about Carter had been almost as unconscionable as lying to herself.

'So what's the favour?' she asked, keen to steer them onto a new, less debilitating topic.

Reese dipped her head towards the trio of guys collected on the other side of the office's grand art deco antechamber—who made a fascinating tableau as they awaited Cassie's arrival with Marnie.

Tuck, Cassie's husband-to-be, stood chatting with his witness, Dylan Brookes. With his rangy athlete's build and tousled blond hair, Tuck looked rugged and gorgeous in a perfectly tailored designer suit, the incessant tapping of his foot on the marble floor the only sign of wedding jitters. Dylan, on the other hand, looked more relaxed and debonair as he kept Tuck's mind off his nerves.

Standing apart from the two close friends, Mason, Reese's ex-husband and current fiancé—and the guy who had effectively stolen her away from Dylan on the eve of their wedding earlier that summer—had his hands buried in the pockets of his suit, the silk tie already tugged loose and listing to one side.

While Dylan was covering any awkwardness with his customary dignity, Mason looked agitated and a little surly. Gina would hazard a guess the ex-marine would rather be charging into a war zone under enemy fire than having to make polite conversation with Reese's former fiancé while wearing a suit.

'I'm about to go rescue Mason, before he rips off his tie altogether—but could you run interference with Dylan later—once Tuck's all loved up with Cassie at the Tribeca.'

Oh, please, just kill me now.

Gina bit the tip of her tongue to stave off the inevitable eye-roll. After her aborted two-week fling in Savannah she wasn't sure she'd be able to flirt again in this lifetime. But how could she mention that to Reese without dragging her friend into her pity party? Which would be pointless in the extreme. What could Reese say about it? Except maybe *I told you so?*

Carter and her had always been a mistake. Even without the miserable secret of the miscarriage lying in wait to trip them up, it never would have worked.

The cold, judgmental look when she'd told him the truth was all the proof she needed that the two of them had never been in line for a happy ever after.

The only thing she hadn't quite accounted for was how horrendous the fallout would be after a measly two weeks with him. And she laid the blame for that squarely at Carter's door. The sex should have been enough for him. But he'd insisted on wanting more, forcing her into an intimacy she couldn't handle, and tricking her into loving him again.

'I can see how it's going to get a little awkward, once you and Mason and Tuck and Cassie are paired off,' Gina observed, trying to concentrate on the problem at hand instead of the insoluble one in her past.

She watched Dylan give Tuck a hearty pat on the back—the two men sharing a joke. 'But I think you may be worrying unnecessarily. Dylan appears to be way too smooth to allow a minor social catastrophe like being jilted at the altar to throw him off his stride.'

'I didn't jilt him,' Reese snapped. 'If you'll recall, he jilted me.' She waved her arm, to dispel the subject. 'But that's beside the point. I don't want him to feel like a fifth wheel at the TriBee. So I could use your super power. If you're sufficiently recovered from the flu, that is?'

The flu—real or imaginary—wouldn't have stopped her before, she thought miserably. Dylan Brookes, with his handsome face, immaculate manners and exceptional dress sense, was exactly the type of guy Gina would once have enjoyed zapping with her super power. But that was before her super power had met its kryptonite in Savannah. A kryptonite that had refused to stay buried.

Carter had attempted to contact her several times since her return home, but she'd deleted his emails and texts unread and erased his answerphone messages—and communicated exclusively with his PA about the commission. Her bags had arrived by special courier the day before with a note attached, addressed in his looping black scrawl, which she'd also thrown away unopened.

She didn't doubt that he had a lot to say to her on the subject of her heartlessness, but she had no desire to get into some long-distance slanging match about the choices she'd made ten years ago. It would only prolong the agony—and, although she despised herself for the weakness, she didn't think she was quite strong enough yet to cope with his contempt—even from a distance of eight hundred miles.

She shook off the depressing thought, and struggled to think of a way to deflect Reese gracefully. 'What about asking Marnic to run interference with your tempting ex? She's young, free and single—and she needs more practice than I do.' She tilted her head as if assessing Dylan's appearance—instead of measuring him against another man she couldn't seem to forget. 'And I bet he'd be her type.'

'You are kidding, right?' Reese did a double take. 'Dylan's exactly the opposite of her type. As you well know Marnie has a phobia of guys who command six-figure salaries and wear tuxes on a regular basis—something to do with the trauma of her debutante upbringing and having them thrown at her on a regular basis.'

Oh, yeah, there was that.

Reese gripped Gina's arm to propel her towards the guys

as Gina silently cursed Marnie and her Post-Traumatic Tux Disorder. 'Come on, there's no need to give him the full Gina today,' she continued, sailing across the marbled hallway in full matchmaker mode. 'We don't want to blind him.'

The blushing bride arrived ten minutes later—in the nick of time to save Gina from slow death by polite conversation. Cassie's low-cut silk dress looked incredible. The silver thread accenting the fabric shimmered in the afternoon light while the snug bias-cut displayed a figure that Cassie had hidden for far too long behind baggy T-shirts and jeans. But it was the expression on Cassie's face as Tuck grasped her waist and swung her around in a circle that had tears threatening to ruin Gina's mascara.

'You look sensational, Cassiopeia!' Tuck announced as his newly crowned Geek Goddess beamed with love and excitement.

The carefree laugh that floated across the antechamber brought forth memories of a certain wicked grin and seductive gaze that had once turned Gina into a giggler too.

She gnawed on her bottom lip—the abject feeling of loss warring with the foolish glow of nostalgia and starting to give her a tension headache.

Thank goodness, she would never lay eyes on Carter Price again or she'd be liable to turn into a complete basketcase.

But as the thought registered it was interrupted by Marnie's choked whisper. 'What's my brother doing here?'

Gina's head snapped up, her startled gaze focusing on a tall figure in a dark business suit weaving his way towards them through the other bridal parties waiting in the antechamber. Her mind steadfastly refused to acknowledge what her eyes were seeing, but as his gaze found hers the heavy weight pressing on her chest began to crush her ribcage.

'Who *is* that guy?' Tuck asked as he sent them all a questioning look. 'He looks pretty mad about something and he's headed this way.'

'That's Carter, Marnie's brother,' Reese said, stating the obvious. 'Did you guys have a meeting?' She turned to Marnie, who shook her head in confusion. He didn't look pretty mad. Gina thought, her chest collapsing, he looked exceptionally mad—and his gaze was locked on her like an Exocet missile.

Cassie sent Gina a sympathetic look. 'I'm not sure it's Marnie he's here to see.'

Gina wrapped her arms around her churning stomach as questions bombarded her from all sides.

'Why is he staring at you, Gina?' Marnie sounded wounded and confused.

'Is something going on between you two, again?' Reese's voice rang out, urgent and concerned.

Gina shook her head but nothing would come out of her mouth. She could feel their worried looks but all she could see was Carter charging towards her and threatening to send her life into freefall again.

'Cassie? Do you know?' Reese's anxious enquiry buzzed in her head.

Before Cassie could reply, Carter marched through the gathered throng and grasped her arm. Yanking her towards him, he snarled, 'Why the hell didn't you answer my emails, or my phone messages, or my damn texts, or the letter I sent with your stuff?'

'Hey, buddy.' Dylan was the first of her shocked friends to come to the rescue—which in some small part of her brain Gina thought was remarkably gallant of him, given that she'd almost bored him to death with her sub-par flirting. 'Do you want to take your hands off the lady and ask her nicely?'

'Butt out, Wall Street,' Carter sneered back, not even sparing him a glance, his Southern manners apparently having gone the same way as his easy charm.

'The hell I will,' Dylan bristled, squaring up for a fight.

'Calm down.' Reese stepped in front of Dylan and touched Gina's arm. 'Gina, is everything okay?'

Gina managed a shell-shocked nod, all her focus on the pads of Carter's fingers digging into her arm, and the glitter of temper in those painfully familiar blue eyes.

What was he doing here? Had he come all this way to humiliate her in front of her friends? Surely she didn't deserve that? She tried to gather her outrage, her indignation, but she couldn't stop trembling.

'L-let go of me,' she stammered, disgusted by the chatter of teeth. To her surprise, his fingers released and he stepped back to thrust a hand through his hair.

Reese puffed out an exasperated breath. 'Now, can someone please tell me what the hell is going on?'

'We need to talk,' Carter said, the tone low as he bypassed Reese's request. 'I didn't plan to do it in public but I will if I have to.'

She tightened her arms, struggling to protect herself from the hard glare. 'No, we don't need to talk.'

She knew what he had to say and she didn't want to hear it. He'd rejected her twice already, once more might break her.

'Fine, you don't want to talk, you can listen.' The frustration in his voice snapped like the lash of a whip.

'Now wait a minute…' Dylan charged back into the fray.

'Who did you say this guy was, because he's starting to make me pretty damn mad too…' Tuck added, standing behind his friend.

'It's okay.' Gina lifted shaking palms to get her knights in shining Armani to back off.

For God's sake, pull yourself together and deal with this, before Cassie's special day degenerates into a complete fiasco.

'I can handle this,' she added, thinking no such thing as the tremor in her body refused to subside.

She could smell him, that unique combination of man and soap and tangy cologne—the memory making the emotion rush through already shaky limbs. She locked her knees in a desperate attempt to keep the trembling under control. 'What is it you wanted to say? I'm listening.'

To her astonishment the glitter of temper disappeared, to leave something she couldn't decipher. He stepped forward and took her arm again but this time his touch was gentle, tentative, the pad of his thumb pressing into the inside of her elbow.

'Let's start with I'm sorry.'

'Sorry? What for?' she asked, staggered.

He dropped his chin to his chest and let out a heavy sigh. 'Damn, this is tough.' He swung his head round, taking in her friends, who were watching with varying degrees of curiosity and astonishment on their faces—and, in Marnie's case, outright shock. 'Especially with an audience,' he added, sucking in a breath as if preparing to face a firing squad.

His hand dropped from her arm. 'Sorry for everything, I guess. Sorry for getting you pregnant that night.'

'What?' Marnie's shocked yelp had him glancing over his shoulder, but he turned his attention back to Gina without acknowledging his sister.

'Sorry for walking away, and letting you think I blamed you for what we did together. Sorry for leaving you to deal with losing our baby alone.' His eyebrow lifted. 'Although, I don't consider myself entirely to blame for that one.'

'How could I tell you when—' she jumped in, but he pressed a fingertip to her lips, silencing her protest.

'Hey, don't. I get it. How could you tell me when I was too busy marrying the wrong woman?'

She looked away, not sure she could hear him say this now, when it was too late to make a difference. She chewed her lip, the metallic taste of blood doing nothing to stop the single tear slipping over her lid. He brushed it away with his thumb, then hooked a finger under her chin.

'You're such a faker, aren't you, sugar? You had me fooled there for a while, with your tough cookie act, but I figured it out.'

She raised her chin, blinking rapidly to stop any more stupid tears materialising. 'Figured out what exactly?'

Damn, she looked so forlorn and so determined not to show a single sign of weakness. How could he ever have doubted the existence of that brave, generous, honest heart behind the tough girl facade?

He'd screwed up. Not just ten years ago by not recognising how perfect she'd always been for him. But also a week ago, when he'd tried to bully her into admitting her feelings, without having the guts to admit his own. He just hoped to hell he wasn't too late to stop those screw-ups from destroying whatever chance they might have at a future.

But he had to tread gently now. She'd had her confidence battered over the years—not just by her old man, but by him too. He'd left her high and dry when she'd needed him the most, because he'd been too busy dealing with his own issues to appreciate what was right under his nose. The news of her miscarriage had been a shock—but once he'd got past the knee-jerk feeling of betrayal, the much bigger shock was how much it had hurt to know she had carried his child and he'd had no idea.

'You want to know my biggest regret, sugar?'

'Not particularly, but I'm sure you're going to tell me anyway.' She sniffed, still channelling the tough cookie act, even though the sheen of moisture in those large green eyes meant it was a total wash.

'My biggest regret is that while I was busy browbeating

you last week into staying in Savannah, I didn't take the time to tell you how I feel about you.'

Now for the tough part.

He gripped her hands and slid down onto one knee.

Her eyes widened in horror as she tugged her wrists, frantically trying to yank him back onto his feet. 'Carter? What the hell are you doing?' she snapped as she sent a panicked 'rescue-me' glance to her friends over his head.

He ignored that, as well as his sister's strangled gasp, the soft whisper of 'Someone pinch me, I think I've been transported into a chick flick,' from Reese, and the Texan growl of 'Who the hell *is* this guy?' from the man he'd recognised from his NFL days as the groom.

'Carter, please, get up, you're making a scene.'

His lips curved at the panicked plea, he was unable to ignore the irony of the situation. Who knew he'd finally get the better of Gina Carrington, not with temper or charm or hot and sweaty sex, but with a cheesy show of sentiment. If this worked out, he was so going to spend the rest of his natural life lavishing her with grand romantic gestures in public places to keep her in line.

'Damn straight I am,' he said, holding onto her wrists and swallowing down the big fat 'if' that had gotten stuck in his throat. 'I'm assuming the position here, because there's something I need to say to you. And this is the only way I know to prove to you I'm sincere.'

Her eyebrows had levitated to her hairline, but she'd stopped trying to free her hands, which he took as a positive sign.

'Right, here goes nothing.' He pressed his thumbs into her wrists and felt the butterfly flutter of her pulse. Even better, she wasn't totally immune.

'I love you, Gina Carrington.' She bucked but he held firm and kept going. 'I love your fire and your passion, your honesty, your integrity, your smart mouth and your bad attitude and that sexy dimple on your butt.'

She gasped and found her voice at last. 'I do not have a dimple on my—'

'I love the way your eyes go all squinty with temper when you're mad,' he interrupted, basking in that exact look. 'And I love the way they go all dazed and dewy when you come.'

'Oh, for Pete's sake!'

'I love the fact that you think you're such a tough cookie. And most of all I love that soft, giving, open heart that you try so hard to keep hidden—but you showed to me one incredible summer night a decade ago, and I've had several tempting glimpses of this summer in Savannah. I'm not a great bet for the long haul, I know that. But then neither are you, so I figure we're even there. And if you'd be willing to take a chance on me, I'm more than ready to take a chance on you.'

He lifted off his knees, cradled her cheeks, so desperate to hold her his body felt as if it were caught in a tractor beam. There was one more thing, though, that had to be said, and it was the hardest of all.

'Now, you can tell me you don't love me and I'll walk out that door and never contact you again.' He stroked her face, willing her to give him another chance. 'But don't lie, sugar. Because I'll know, and then I'll just have to get back on my knees and embarrass us both all over again.'

He could hear the hush of anticipation, not only from her friends but from the sizeable crowd in the hall who'd all been silenced by his declaration.

She swallowed audibly. 'Do you have any idea how much I want to kick your butt at this moment, Carter Price?'

The grin spread across his face—and his heart—because he could hear the hitch in that sultry purr, and knew he'd struck gold. 'You didn't just answer my question with another question, did you, sugar?'

A small laugh choked out through the tears tumbling down her cheeks. Then she flung her arms around his neck and whispered into his hair. 'I love you too, Rhett. But I'm still going to kick your butt the first chance I get.'

Spontaneous applause broke out around the hall as he covered her lips with his and sank into the long-awaited kiss.

When they were both forced to come up for air, he held her at arm's length and said with a smile that he was pretty sure reached both ears simultaneously, 'Frankly, my dear, I'd enjoy watching you try.'

After all the drama, Cassie and Tuck's wedding went off like a dream. The bride saying her vows in a sure, steady voice and then turning to smile at her friends once Tuck had said his.

Gina had to be grateful that Carter's warm palm anchored her hip to his side throughout the ceremony, or she would surely have floated off on a cloud of bliss. His insane declaration in front of half of Manhattan had terrified her at first, but as his words sank into her consciousness the strangest thing had happened—the panicked beat of her heart had slowed, the lead weight in her stomach had dissolved and all those barriers that she'd spent so many years erecting and maintaining had come tumbling down in one fell swoop.

She laid her head on Carter's shoulder in one of the limousines Reese had booked to transport them to Cassie's reception party, and listened to Carter chat easily to Dylan—the two of them having developed mutual amnesia about their earlier stand-off, like typical guys. Staring into space, she used the moment of calm to contemplate the difficult decisions in her future.

Carter had invited himself back to her place tonight and told her he'd organised a week's leave from the Mill, but the eight hundred miles that separated them were going to be the first obstacle they'd have to discuss.

But as the car cruised through the early evening traffic, and she watched the office workers flooding into the subway to begin the Labor Day weekend, she had a sudden yearning for the subtle pace and relaxed gentility of Savannah. While she'd once thrived on the manic energy of the City That Never Sleeps, it didn't seem quite so necessary any more, now she was embarking on a relationship that promised to generate enough energy to fuel a nuclear power plant.

Marnie sat on the other side of the limo, her unfocused gaze fixed on something out of the window, but when her eyes flicked to her brother and then back out of the window Gina knew the siblings' strained relationship was going to be a much bigger hurdle to overcome than her living arrangements.

The Tribeca Terrace was everything they had wanted in a surprise party venue. Reese had put her organisational skills to work on the ride over, ensuring an extra place setting for Carter appeared as if by magic amid the balloons, streamers and the enormous Just Hitched banner she'd already arranged to adorn their table.

Gina's thanks for her friend's thoughtfulness was greeted with a cocked eyebrow. 'Don't think I've forgotten your gross dereliction of shag and share duty. If he's not the Mystery Studmuffin, I'll eat my Jimmy Choos.' But then she added in a soft murmur that had Gina repairing her mascara again, 'I'm thrilled for you two. After all the heartache you've both been through, you deserve this chance.'

As the evening progressed Gina found her flirt gene shimmering happily back to life under Carter's heavily lidded gaze—the desire to race back to her apartment and tear his clothes off becoming increasingly imperative. But as they swayed together on the restaurant's small dance floor, the slow rub of his body against hers making her throat dry, she noticed Marnie pouring herself a hefty glass of Chardonnay while Dylan sat opposite her, engrossed in his smartphone.

Pulling Carter's head down by the ears, she whispered, 'You need to speak to your sister. Sort things out with her.'

He nuzzled her neck. 'I don't need Marnie's permission and neither do you.'

Gina sighed, forced to file 'fixing his relationship with his sister' into a folder marked 'works in progress'—Carter's response making it blatantly obvious that his relationship with his sister seemed to have arrested somewhere around Marnie's eighteenth birthday.

Her thoughts scattered completely when his hands drifted down to her butt: 'I suggest you save your freak out about Marnie for another time,' he murmured, giving her backside a proprietary squeeze. 'Because you've got something a lot bigger to handle tonight, sugar.'

The husky giggle, which was never far from the surface now, bubbled out as his hips brushed against hers—and the casual endearment settled around her like a golden fog.

She'd never considered herself a sweet person, but somehow Carter Price's good opinion had managed to shear off a lot of her sour edges and—while shedding that protective layer of sarcasm altogether would have to be another 'work in progress'—she couldn't wait to discover her inner Pollyanna.

Fisting her fingers into his hair, she dragged his mouth down to hers.

That said, she didn't intend to let true love turn her into a total sucker.

'Oh, don't you worry, Rhett.' She pressed provocatively against the rather prominent bulge in his suit pants. 'I think I've got the measure of you,' she purred, delighted when his heartfelt groan was followed by an exceptionally sinful kiss.

* * * * *

T